HORSES AND HEATHER

What this story is about:

Christine and Colin Scott, and their cousin, Alison, had been invited to spend the summer holidays with Edna Blythe who kept a small riding school near the sea. They arrived at the stables one foggy day to find that Edna had been taken to hospital, leaving no one in charge of the horses. When they had recovered from the unpleasant surprise, they decided that they were quite capable of looking after the riding school, and immediately set to work.

The rest of the story tells of the adventures and mishaps they shared with a happy-go-lucky Irishman, and points out the difficulties as well as the pleasures of looking after horses.

HORSES and HEATHER

by GILLIAN BAXTER

Illustrated by Sheila Rose

FREDERICK WARNE & CO. LTD.
LONDON AND NEW YORK

Printed in Great Britain

CONTENTS

Chapter One

LEFT IN CHARGE

ALISON DALBY peered frantically through the fog outside the train window in an attempt to see the name of the station.

"Well, are we there?" asked her cousin, Colin Scott, impatiently.

"I can't see a thing," replied Alison, rubbing the misty window.

"Here, get out of the way," ordered Christine Scott, pushing her young cousin away from the window, and opening it as the train slid to a halt.

"Is this Stone Crossing?" she asked the dim shape of a hurrying porter.

"Aye, that's right," agreed the man, vanishing into the fog.

The children hurled themselves, their luggage, and their dog out on to the platform, expecting the train to move off at any moment. Irritatingly it remained still. The dog, a Jack Russell terrier called Punch, had managed to get his lead tangled round the nearest case, and was pulling back in an attempt to free himself. Alison tried to untangle him without much success, as he kept struggling and making the tangle worse. In the end Colin

7

had to help her, and at last they were ready to look for some way of reaching their destination.

The three had been invited to spend the summer holidays with Edna Blythe, an old friend of Colin's and Christine's mother, who owned a small riding school near Stone Crossing, in reach of the sea.

They found the exit in the thick sea mist with difficulty, and asked the ticket collector where they could get the bus for Stone Heath where the riding school was. He explained, and they made their way to the station yard, where after searching for a time they discovered the bus stop.

They had half an hour to wait, but they did not dare to venture far as they were certain that they would get lost, and be unable to find the bus stop again in the mist.

At last a small, ancient single-decker bus arrived, and they piled in, Punch exchanging growls and glares with a small, fat scottie who was just inside. They asked the conductor to tell them when they reached Stone Heath, and tried to see something of the country through the windows. But the mist was too thick for them to see more than hedges or fences, and narrow strips of grass or crops inside them. Before long the hedges and fences gave way to heath land, and soon the bus stopped.

"You're there," the conductor said. "The stables are down that path."

He pointed into the mist, and they made out dimly a narrow sandy path leading off across the heath.

After thanking him, the three started off through the mist, Punch trailing dismally at their heels. He did not approve of this walk. It was wet and uncomfortable, and the country was strange.

They walked for about five minutes, and then a fence loomed up out of the fog, and they saw the dark mass of a cottage. Alison spotted a gate, beside which was a board and on it was painted:

STONE HEATH RIDING SCHOOL

HUNTERS, PONIES, AND HACKS FOR HIRE.

CHILDREN A SPECIALITY.   PONIES FOR SALE.

LIVERIES TAKEN

"Obviously, we've arrived," said Colin, when they had read this.

They pushed open a white painted, five-barred gate, and found themselves in a yard. On one side stood the dark mass that was the house, and in front of them were more dark shapes, obviously stables. There was a sweet smell of horses, hay, and leather, and the faint, strange smell of Radiol Embrocation, which seemed nearly to blot everything else out.

Hearing their footsteps a dog began to bark, and after a moment a lanky young Dalmatian appeared out of the fog.

Punch growled, and the Dalmatian bounced up gaily, wagging its long tail and barking. But no one appeared to greet them.

9

"That's odd," remarked Alison.

"Let's go up to the house," suggested Christine.

They found their way round to the side door, and Christine knocked. There was no reply. She tried again, and then they found their way round to the front door, and again Christine knocked. Still no reply.

They returned to the side door, and Alison tried it. To her surprise it opened.

"Shall we go in?" asked Christine. "I suppose it is the right house?"

"Of course it is, what else could it be?" asked Colin. "We had better go in. Miss Blythe may be ill or something."

They entered the house, and found themselves standing in the kitchen. A slow-burning stove made the room almost unbearably hot, and the table was still laid for breakfast.

"Is anyone in?" shouted Alison.

There was no answer.

Then Christine saw the envelope on the table. It was addressed to them all. She picked it up, and drew out the single sheet of paper which it contained, and read aloud:

Dear children,

I have appendicitis and have been taken to hospital. A friend of mine should have arrived before you do, to take charge of the horses. Please make yourselves at home. I will arrange for someone to

10

come and look after you as soon as possible, but I am afraid it will not be until to-morrow. There are eggs, ham, and lettuce in the 'fridge, and bread in the safe. I am in Midgely hospital.

Yours,

EDNA BLYTHE.

It was dated that day.

"Well!" gasped Christine.

"I didn't see anyone outside," remarked Colin.

"We wouldn't, in that fog," replied Alison.

"Well, let's go out and see if anyone is there," suggested Christine.

They left their luggage in the kitchen, and ventured out into the mist. They crossed the yard in the direction of the buildings and were greeted by eager whinnies.

"Anyone about?" shouted Colin.

The Dalmatian barked, but there was no other reply. Then the stables loomed up through the mist. There was a row of three loose boxes, and a long, enclosed shed, from which came bangs and whinnies. Out of the box at the end farthest from the shed appeared a bay head with a blaze. It belonged to a big bay thoroughbred, of about sixteen two hands. He banged his door eagerly with a forefoot, and craned out.

Alison looked into his box. He had not been mucked out, and his water bucket was dry. An empty hay net hung beside his manger, and his light, checked summer sheet had slipped sideways, and trailed on the ground.

11

In the next box stood a dark, almost liver-chestnut mare, who looked like a part bred Arab. She, too, hung over her door and called to them.

In the last box stood a hogged grey hunter, with a sensible head, a roman nose, long tail, and darkly dappled quarters. The children soon saw that none of them were mucked out, and they all needed water. There was no sign of anyone in the yard.

"They must have been held up by the fog," said Alison, leaving the bay, whose sheet she had been straightening.

"Let's investigate the sheds," suggested Christine.

They pulled open the half door, and entered the long, wooden building with its corrugated iron roof, and cement floor. It was divided into about twelve stalls, only two of which were occupied—one by a fat chestnut pony with a white face, who stood about thirteen hands high, the other by a sleek little bay mare of fourteen hands. In a stall at the end were stored ten trusses of mixture hay, and in a feed bin they discovered chaff, bran, and oats. There was also a tin of linseed.

"Well, we had better start work," said Alison, when they had explored.

"First we shall have to change our clothes," said Christine firmly, with visions of Alison starting to muck out in her new grey coat, one of her best cotton frocks, and new white sandals.

Christine led the other two back to the cottage, and

they set out in search of their rooms. They found three bedrooms, one of which obviously belonged to Edna Blythe. One of the others contained twin beds, both of which were made up, and in the last room stood one bed, also made up. They climbed more stairs and found themselves in a well-furnished attic room.

"This must belong to Miss Blythe's friend," said Christine. "Mummy said that she had gone away for the summer."

They returned to their own rooms, and changed hurriedly into jodhpurs. Alison turned her case out all over her bed. She had chosen the one nearest to the window, changed in about three seconds, and would have dashed straight out to the stables if Christine had not caught her, and ordered her to hang up her coat and frocks.

This took Alison only a few minutes, and Christine was almost as quick. Five minutes later they were back in the kitchen where they had left Punch. He was very glad to see them, and almost tripped them up with excitement as they hurried towards the door.

"What about lunch?" asked Christine suddenly. "It's half past one now."

"Oh, bother lunch!" replied Alison, throwing the door open.

"But . . . " began Christine.

But Colin and Alison had gone, and Christine followed, deciding to get lunch later when the horses were

13

done. As she was seventeen, three years older than Colin, and four years older than Alison, she felt responsible.

They made their way through the mist to the stables, and began to search for water, pitchforks, brooms, straw, and anything else that they might need.

Christine found the pitchforks and brooms in the shed, and Colin discovered a tap and trough at the side of the loose boxes. But they could not find the straw anywhere until Alison, suddenly having a brainwave, found it in what they had thought to be the coal shed, but which turned out to be two small sheds together, one containing straw and the other, the tack.* The coal was heaped behind them.

They set to work first watering, then mucking out. They found head collars in the tack room, and decided to tie the horses up until they knew them better. The bay was the only one who seemed at all difficult. He laid back his ears and threatened to kick when Christine approached him, and snapped at her when she tied him up. His feet always seemed to be on the straw which she wanted to move, and he was very grudging about moving over. Alison, next door in the chestnut mare's box, was having an easier time. The mare moved over easily, and was very friendly. Alison fell in love with her at once.

Colin, who was doing the grey, also found him docile. He was an elderly horse, his legs scarred from the hunting field, but with good hocks and quarters. Colin

*A stable word for saddlery; an abbreviation of tackle.

imagined that he was a good ride, and the sort of horse who would be there to the end, and still ready for the hack home.

When Alison mucked out both ponies, she discovered that the chestnut nipped, and the bay was friendly.

Colin and Christine bedded down all five, and filled the hay nets belonging to the two horses. The ponies did not appear to have hay nets, and so they filled the hay racks.

"We'd better not give them short feeds. We should probably give them the wrong amounts," said Christine, as they hayed the last pony.

"I wonder what their names are," said Alison, staring thoughtfully at the chestnut mare.

"Let's see if they're up in the tack room anywhere," suggested Christine.

"What about lunch though? I'm starving," said Colin.

"We'll get something," replied Christine. "Come on Alison."

She dragged her unwilling cousin into the house, leaving Colin to put the head collars away in the tack room.

Five of the saddles and bridles were obviously in regular use. The rest were dusty. There were ten saddles and twelve bridles altogether. There were names written on cards, and pinned under the saddle brackets. Albatross, Springheeled Jack, Oberon, Puck, Melody, Golden Chord, and Trix. Colin wondered which was which.

15

There were too many names for the number of horses, and he wondered uneasily if they had missed any that were kept elsewhere. But looking back at the dusty tack he decided that it was more likely that the others had been sold, or were no longer at Stone Heath.

Then he heard Christine calling, and he ran through the fog to the house. The mist seemed to be lifting a little. It seemed lighter, and he noticed that the stables were visible from the side door, and he could just see the outline of the fence beyond the sheds.

Christine and Alison prepared fried ham and eggs, and discovered some tins of fruit. They had opened a tin of peaches, and some cream. By that time it was half past two.

The three ate hungrily, and finished everything while they discussed what to do. They could not go home as their parents were in France.

"We shall have to stay," said Colin. "We do know something about horses, anyway, and someone will have to look after them."

"Besides, where else can we go?" asked Alison.

"There's Aunt Mavis," suggested Christine dubiously. Aunt Mavis was not really an aunt. She was a distant cousin who lived in Bournemouth, and her hobby was breeding miniature poodles.

"Christine, we couldn't," cried Alison. "We'd spend the entire holidays exercising poodles on the promenade."

"I agree with her," said Colin. "It would be awful."

"We can't go. Your Mother said that Aunt Mavis had gone away for a holiday herself," Alison suddenly remembered. "She's left the kennel maids to look after the poodles for her."

"Yes, of course," Christine felt that she ought not to be so glad. "Well, I suppose we shall have to stay then."

Chapter Two

THEIR FIRST CUSTOMERS

THEY were all helping with the washing up after their meal, when they heard the Dalmatian barking, and a knock came at the side door.

Alison opened it and found two children, a girl of about twelve, and a boy of about seven, standing outside, dressed in jodhpurs and hard hats.

"We're riding at three," announced the girl, who had red hair and freckles. "Where's Miss Blythe?"

Alison explained.

"Oh well, you'll have to take us out then," said the girl cheerfully.

"But we don't know any of the rides," argued Christine, who had come to listen. "Or anything about these horses. We don't even know their names."

"That doesn't matter. I do," replied the girl. "I'm Elsie Downs. This is Harry, my brother."

"What shall we do?" asked Christine.

"Well, the mist is a lot clearer," replied Colin. "I think we'd better take them. After all, if they know the rides it should be all right."

"Do you know the rides?" asked Christine.

"Of course. I've been riding here for a year," replied Elsie.

"All right then. What do you usually ride?" asked Christine.

"Harry has Puck," replied Elsie. She looked at Christine for a moment, and then said, "And I have Trix."

"Which are they?" asked Christine, not suspecting anything. She did wonder why Harry was wearing a broad grin, but she did not remark on it.

"Puck's the pony with the white face," replied Elsie. "And Trix is the dark chestnut."

"Who'll take them?" asked Alison.

"I will," replied Christine. "I'm the oldest, and so if anything goes wrong, it had better be with me."

They all went down to the tack room, and Christine said, "What shall I ride?"

"The grey?" suggested Colin. "You're too big for the bay pony really."

"If you mean Albatross, he only has walking exercise," said Elsie. "He's been lame. Miss Blythe's been rubbing him with embrocation."

"Well, either the thoroughbred, or the pony then," said Christine. "I'd better take the pony. The horse looks a handful."

"Miss Blythe doesn't like heavy people on Melody," said Elsie, looking at Christine's five feet seven thoughtfully.

"It surely wouldn't hurt Melody for once," answered

Christine. "I only weigh just over nine stone."

"Miss Blythe wouldn't like it. She doesn't like people over eight stone on Melody," replied Elsie.

"Then you had better have her, and I'll have Trix," suggested Christine.

"I like Trix better," replied Elsie sulkily.

"Oh, all right. I'll try the bay," replied Christine impatiently.

"He's called Springheeled Jack," Elsie informed her.

They collected the three sets of tack, and went to saddle up. Puck wore a single reined pelham, and a well-made small saddle. Trix had a snaffle bridle with a dropped noseband, and a worn, comfortable looking hunting saddle. Jack had an almost new, beautifully made saddle, with the flaps cut rather far forward, a sheepskin numnah, a running martingale and a vulcanite pelham.

"Is Harry on the lead?" asked Colin, leading Puck out of the shed.

"No. He's been riding for about a year," replied Elsie, who was mounting Trix with Alison's help.

When her two riders were safely up, Christine led Jack out. Colin gave her a leg up, and she adjusted her stirrups while he held the bay's head. Jack refused to stand. He swung round and round, and shook his head trying to get away from Colin.

"All right?" asked Colin at last.

"Yes, I think so," replied Christine, gathering up her reins properly.

Jack tried to spring forward the moment Colin let him go, and Christine had difficulty in keeping him back while she waited for the two children. Elsie was looking slightly doubtful now that she was up, but Trix looked calm enough, and Christine led the way out. Jack refused to walk, but jogged sideways down the path, shaking his head about, and trying to canter.

"Which way?" asked Christine.

"Straight on, then across the road, and into the birch wood," replied Elsie.

The mist was a lot thinner, but they could still see only about three hundred yards ahead, and Christine wondered if she had been mad to agree to take them. Jack felt terribly fresh, and his back was right up. He was very big, and felt uncomfortably strong. His rather long ears were sharply pricked, his tail was arched. He threw his feet about, and tried to jerk his head down, giving little hops which could quite easily turn into proper bucks.

Then they reached the road, and had to stop while a car and a jeep passed. This irritated Jack thoroughly, and he plunged across the road at a canter as soon as Christine told him to walk on. She pulled him up on the other side, and heard a scuffle behind her. Trix was cantering sideways, her nose in the air, and Elsie was hanging on to her mane with one hand, and holding her reins very short with the other. Puck squealed, and shot past her.

"Lengthen your reins. Sit up, and let go of the mane,"

21

ordered Christine, as Jack gave a leap sideways in mock fright.

Christine lost a stirrup, and dropped a rein. Jack took advantage of it, and bucked. Christine hung on somehow, and managed to pull his head up. Behind her, Trix kicked out at Puck, who almost brushed Harry off against a tree trying to avoid her heels.

Jack plunged, and almost pulled the reins out of Christine's hands again. Then a backfire from the road behind them sent Trix into a bucking fit. Elsie fell off, and Trix dived past Jack, who was plunging furiously, kicking out at him as she passed, and her stirrups flying, and her reins trailing round her feet, she vanished into the mist.

Puck squealed, and jumped into the air, and Harry slid off hurriedly, and hung on to him. The chestnut pony, longing to follow Trix, almost pulled Harry over in his attempts to get away.

Jack was bucking and plunging wildly, his eyes on the place where Trix had vanished. Christine was uncomfortably aware that she was on no pony now, but a fit, fresh thoroughbred. He plunged again, leaping forward, almost getting away from her, and Christine realised that she could not hold him much longer. She thought of getting off, but he was throwing himself about too much. Then he gave two large stiff legged leaps, and was off down the narrow ride between the birch trees.

Christine pulled vainly on the reins. The big bay had his head between his knees, and he had forgotten that she was on his back. Behind her, Puck tried even harder to follow, but Harry managed to hang on to him. Elsie began to run down the ride after the vanishing bay.

Christine was terrified. The trees seemed horribly close. They scraped her knees, and Jack seemed to miss

them by inches. Before her the ride stretched on, reddish sand between the green and silver trees, and the short, brilliant patches of turf.

There was no sign of Trix. Jack shied at a shadow,

kicked out lightheartedly, and dashed on. Christine had lost both her stirrups, and she was hanging on to the bay's mane most of the time. Then, through the thinning mist, she saw the trees end. Before her was open heathland, heathery and rough, with many hillocks and outbreaks of stone. The ride went on, joining several others. The heath seemed patched with them. Jack turned sharply to the left, and tore on.

Christine managed to collect her reins again, and began to try everything she could think of to stop. Short pulls, long pulls, each rein in turn, and at last he was slowing. She gave another tug, and he dropped into a trot at last. He was hardly sweating, and his breathing seemed to be easy. Christine got him back into a walk, and wondered what to do next. Should she go back to her riders, or look for Trix?

She decided on the former. Elsie might be hurt, or Puck might prove too much for Harry to hang on to.

She turned Jack round, and started back down the ride, following her horse's hoofprints. The mist had almost gone, but it still hung a little in the hollows and among the trees. She scanned the purple and brown landscape for Trix. The mist caught and held the light, making everything dazzling. Above, the sky was a clear, hot blue. Everything was dripping, and the ground steamed, adding to the remaining mist. Jack was jogging, and snatching at his bit. Then, right over among the heather, Christine spotted the chestnut mare. She was almost the colour of the landscape, but as Christine watched, she moved, and Jack had seen her too.

He pricked his long ears, and Christine felt him shake all over as he whinnied. He bounced excitedly, and she hoped that he would not take off again. But she managed to keep him in a jogging walk, and turned down the nearest ride that seemed to lead towards Trix. She might as well try to catch the mare now that she had seen her.

Trix saw her coming and walked towards her, ears pricked, whickering to Jack, who jogged sideways, and answered her with a shrill whinny. Trix came right up, ignoring Christine, and reached out her nose to the big bay. Christine reached across to grab the reins, but Trix squealed coyly and jumped back. Gingerly, Christine edged Jack alongside the chestnut. Trix didn't move. Christine hung out of the saddle, and managed to get Trix's reins just in time. Caught! But the chestnut was suddenly friendly. She rubbed her nose against Christine's knee, and led quietly as Christine turned Jack round and rode towards the woods. Then she saw Elsie coming down the ride to meet her. They met by the woods, and Christine dismounted.

"Are you all right?" she asked.

"Yes," replied Elsie. "I'm sorry I let her go."

"She seems to be all right, except for her reins," Christine told her. "Do you think you could manage to ride her back to the stables?"

"I'll try," replied Elsie.

25

Christine knotted Trix's broken reins, and helped Elsie to mount. Then she managed to remount Jack whilst he nibbled at a bush, and led the way back to Harry, who was still holding Puck's reins, and watching him eat.

He scrambled on again without any help, and Christine said that she thought they had better get back to the stables before anything else happened. The hour was almost up anyway.

Elsie did not seem particularly sorry, but Harry looked miserable. Christine remembered that he had only walked, and had not even followed Trix.

"Would you like to canter to the end of the ride?" she asked him. "Stop well before you reach the road."

"Oh good!" Harry pushed Puck past Jack into the lead. "Are you coming Elsie?" he asked.

"No," replied Elsie shortly.

Harry kicked Puck energetically but inelegantly, and trotted on down the ride. It took a good deal of kicking and waving of legs on Harry's part before Puck condescended to canter slowly and bumpily for a few yards.

Jack bounced eagerly, but Christine managed to hold him back. Trix squealed, and tried to shoot past him, but Christine grabbed her reins as she came level. She led the chestnut the rest of the way down the ride to where Harry waited for them by the road with Puck, who was eating happily again.

This time the stables could be seen properly as the mist had cleared, and Christine saw that they stood quite alone. Behind the stable buildings was a small paddock, in which stood some things that looked like jumps. The buildings were surrounded by heathland, and in the distance they could see the deep blue of the sea. Away to one side was the village.

They were about to cross the road when a car came round the corner of the woods, and on seeing them, stopped dead with a piercing squeal of brakes that made Jack and Trix shy and plunge.

The driver opened the door, and got out.

"What in the world do you think you're doing on my horse, young lady?" he bellowed at Christine.

"Your horse?" gasped Christine. "What on earth are you talking about? He comes from the Stone Heath Riding School."

"Of course he does. I stable him there," snapped the man. "Did Miss Blythe tell you to ride him?"

"No. She's in hospital with appendicitis," replied Christine.

"I see. And who might you be?" asked the man.

"Christine Scott. I'm staying at the stables with my brother and cousin," answered Christine.

"Oh, are you," said the man grimly. "And what might you be doing on Trix, Elsie Downs?" he went on.

"Riding her," replied Elsie.

It was obvious that she was used to Jack's formidable owner.

"Why?" asked the man.

"I wanted to, and Miss Scott said I could," replied Elsie.

"But did Miss Scott know that you hadn't ridden her before?" asked the man.

"No," admitted Elsie.

"Did you manage her all right?" he asked.

"No. She bucked me off," Elsie replied.

"And how did you like my Jack?" his owner asked Christine.

"I couldn't stop him," replied Christine reluctantly. "But he's a lovely horse."

The man laughed, to her great relief.

"Of course you couldn't stop him," he told her. "I have a job with him. He's corned up for show jumping, and he didn't go out yesterday."

"I'm sorry, I didn't know he was a livery*," Christine told him.

"That's all right. You don't appear to have harmed him, and he doesn't appear to have harmed you. You had better get him back to the stables though," Jack's owner told her.

Christine obeyed, and the three horses crossed the road and approached the stables, the car turning into the track behind them, and following slowly at a distance.

Hearing their hooves as they entered the yard, Colin and Alison dashed to meet them, and Albatross whinnied.

"How did it go?" shouted Colin, running across the

*Boarder at the stable.

yard with the Dalmatian leaping round him, making Jack shy.

"I'll tell you in a minute," replied Christine. "The man in the car is Jack's owner."

"Help!" exclaimed Alison. "Is he a full livery?"

"Yes," replied Christine, sliding off Jack.

"How did Trix break her reins?" inquired Alison, taking her from Elsie.

"She bucked me off and trod on them," replied Elsie.

"You had a good ride," said Colin sarcastically, taking Puck from Harry.

Jack's owner parked his car by the tack room, and came across to the bay's box, where Christine was busy unsaddling him. He was a tall, stern looking man, with greying dark hair and grey eyes. He looked as though he had been in the army.

"Did Elsie Downs tell you that she always rode Trix?" he asked, unfastening Jack's folded leather girth.

"Not exactly, but that was the impression she gave," Christine told him, unfastening the curb chain, and slipping the bridle over Jack's long, bay ears.

"She's always wanted to, but Edna wouldn't let her," said the man, lifting the saddle and numnah off Jack's back, and folding the girth across it. "Trix always bucks a bit, but she's so showy. Perhaps this will cure Elsie for a bit, Not for long, I'm afraid. She's not the sort of child to be put off for long by a fall. She should make a good rider some day."

"What does she usually ride?" asked Christine. "Melody?"

"Yes, or Albatross when he's sound, or one of the heath ponies."

"Heath ponies?" asked Christine.

"Yes. Edna has five running out on the heath," explained the man. "There are a lot of ponies out there, belonging to various people nearby. It's run rather like the New Forest—round ups twice a year, and all the ponies branded. Some people have twenty or more out. There's a lot of the heath. It goes on for miles. Edna's five are two unbroken three-year-olds, a mare with a foal, and two other ponies, a chestnut and a brown. Puck and Melody both have her brand. They take turns with the others running out."

"Oh, so that's who Golden Chord and Oberon are," said Christine, who was rubbing Jack's saddle mark with clean straw. He was not very hot, but he was still wet under the saddle.

"Yes," agreed the man. "Oberon's the brown pony, Golden Chord the chestnut. They are nice animals—the showier type of heath pony."

He picked up Jack's tack, and left the box. Elsie appeared in his place.

"I'm sorry I told you I rode Trix," she said. "And I should have told you about Jack. But it's true about Melody, her front legs aren't very good, and she's getting old. I thought if you knew about Jack you'd have to ride Trix, and then I couldn't have done."

"That's all right Elsie," Christine told her. "But for goodness' sake don't do anything like that again. You might hurt yourself or the horse badly, if you found that you couldn't manage it after all."

"I know, I'm sorry," repeated Elsie.

"When are you coming again?" asked Christine, to change the subject.

"On Friday," said Elsie. "That's in two days."

"All right. Do you know where Miss Blythe keeps the bookings?" asked Christine.

"Yes, I'll get the book," offered Elsie. She dashed off, and Christine examined Jack's feet for stones, put on his sheet, and left the box. His owner was crossing the yard towards her.

"I thought I'd better explain the feeding the different ponies get," he explained. "I'll write it out."

He took a small note-book and a fountain pen out of his pocket, rested it on the top of Jack's door, and began to write. He wrote for about five minutes, tore out the two pages that he had covered, and handed them to Christine. He had put down the name of each pony, the amount of feed, and the feeding times.

Later he led the three down to the shed, and showed them Puck's and Melody's brands, a simple "E.B."

"She would have used only one initial, but both 'E.' and 'B.' are in use separately already," he explained. "By the way, Albatross has an hour's walking exercise each day, and no oats. He's recovering from a strained tendon. If you keep up the embrocation, and the steady exercise, he should be right again soon. He is sound already, but the vet wants to be quite certain before he starts normal work again. By the way, my name's Davidson. Robert Davidson."

"Did you want to take Jack out?" asked Christine. "I'm sorry I rode him."

"That's all right. I didn't really want to ride him to-day. I haven't time. But I thought he'd have to go out. I had better go now, as I haven't got to ride him. I'll be over to-morrow."

He went back to his car, turned round expertly judging the distances with the ease of long practice, and vanished down the track. Colin closed the gate behind him, and called the Dalmatian, who was chasing the car.

"His name's Prunes," Elsie informed him, hearing him calling, "Dog."

Colin yelled "Prunes," and the Dalmatian came haring back, his long legs carrying him very fast, and almost tripping him up. Punch was yapping excitedly by the gate, and both dogs tore round the yard barking, almost knocking Alison over.

"What does it say about feeding?" Colin asked, seeing Christine reading the notes with interest.

"Jack has eight pounds of oats a day, in three feeds," replied Christine. "Trix has five pounds, Albatross none, just chaff and bran, and the ponies two each."

"All in three feeds?" asked Colin.

"Yes. At eight, one and five," replied Christine. "They have hay nets filled in the morning and at five."

"We had better start straightening the beds, and watering," remarked Alison, arriving from the direction of the tack room in time to hear Christine reading the feeding times. "It's half past four now."

The other two agreed, and they set to work, Elsie helping willingly, and Harry playing with the dogs.

"Don't throw stones for them," begged Christine, noticing him. "They'll swallow them or something."

Harry chose a piece of wood instead, and Punch raced after Prunes, yapping with excitement, but never quite catching him.

They finished the beds and watering, and Alison replenished the hay nets for the night while Christine and Colin fed the short feed.

Elsie showed them where the embrocation was kept, and in which leg Albatross had been lame, so that Christine could attend to it. Then Elsie and Harry, who lived in the neighbouring village, went home and the other three shut up the stables for the night, locking the tack room, and making sure that all the doors were safe, before going into the house to find some supper. They had to finish washing up the lunch things first, which they had completely forgotten when Elsie and Harry had arrived during the afternoon, and then search the cupboards and 'fridge for something to eat. They finally opened some more tins as there seemed to be nothing else, and had tomato soup, spaghetti, and bread and cheese. Then, after tidying up, they went upstairs to finish unpacking properly.

It was while they were unpacking that the doorbell rang, and, dashing down, Colin opened the door to find a rather sheepish looking boy of about nineteen standing on the step. He was dressed in breeches and Wellington boots, and an old bicycle leaned against the wall beside him.

"I'm John Cary," he announced. "Miss Blythe asked me to do her horses to-day seeing as she was ill, but I had a puncture, and then the fog was so thick I didn't think I'd find the way—we're away across the heath you see—so I waited until it cleared." He paused for breath, and Colin said, "It's all right, we did the horses. We've come to stay here, and we can do them again to-morrow, so you needn't come if you've got too much to do."

"We are busy," agreed the boy. "We're that short handed, and the milking machine's gone wrong, so it's all got to be done by hand. You're sure you can manage though?"

"Yes, we enjoy it," replied Colin.

"Then I'll get back. I'm sorry I didn't get here earlier." The boy collected his bicycle, and prepared to ride away. "If you should need any help, I come from Cliff Farm. Anyone in the village will show you the way."

He clanked away down the rough, stony lane, and Colin dashed back upstairs to tell the others who had called.

"What a good thing we came," said Alison, when he had finished.

"And now we *can't* go home, or anywhere else," remarked Colin.

"Hurrah," cried Alison. "We shall get bags of riding."

"There'll by plenty of work as well," Colin told her. "We shall probably not get much time over for riding."

"Someone's got to take the rides though," Alison reminded him. "And we shan't have to work all the time. There are only five horses."

"It'll certainly be fun," agreed Colin.

Chapter Three

※※

BECOMING ORGANISED

NEXT morning Alison woke very early. Her watch said six-thirty, but the sun was already streaming in through the thin curtains, and she decided to get up.

She dressed without waking Christine, and crept downstairs. Punch bounded across the kitchen to meet her, and Prunes stood up and stretched.

Alison found some biscuits in the cupboard, took a handful, and opened the door letting in the sweet, fresh air of an early summer morning. The dogs dashed out, and flew across the yard barking. Jack whinnied. Alison went across to the boxes, and gave Trix a biscuit. Then she looked round. Everywhere she looked was the purple heath, dotted with small coppices and woods, with rocky outcrops and sandy patches between the heather and turf. Not far away grazed several ponies, and Alison decided to walk towards them and see if they were Miss Blythe's other horses.

She whistled the dogs, and they came racing after her, falling over each other in their haste, and bounding round her in circles.

As she drew nearer to them she saw that there were seven ponies in the group, two chestnuts, one red and one

36

golden, three browns, a bay, and a grey. One of the browns and the bay had foals at their sides.

Seeing her coming, the ponies raised their heads. The golden chestnut whinnied, and took a couple of steps towards her, the others just watched. The red

chestnut and the grey were obviously youngsters, still rather leggy with bushy, wild manes and tails and wide, startled eyes. The red chestnut was the showiest, with his brilliant coat, small, slightly Arabian head, and lovely forehand. The grey was not quite so good looking, but she had a nice head, and a short back. The golden chestnut was older, almost a show pony type, with a very light golden coat, flaxen mane and tail, white socks in front, and a star. One of the browns was a nice looking gelding of about thirteen hands, another, an elderly mare with a small dun foal, and the third a nice, solid type of pony. The bay mare was nice looking, but when she moved Alison saw that she was lame. Her foal was brown, and looked older than the dun.

All but the golden chestnut moved away a little as Alison approached, but the little mare waited, ears pricked, nostrils flaring. Alison held out her hand with a small piece of broken biscuit on it, and the mare waited. She had the brand "E.B." on her flank. Looking beyond her, Alison saw that the others also carried Miss Blythe's brand, except the bay and the solid brown, who both carried a "K".

Golden Chord accepted the biscuit, and allowed Alison to slide an arm round her neck and catch her. Alison led her a few steps, patted her, and let her go. She approached the others, but they moved away, breaking into a trot as she persisted. Golden Chord watched them for a moment, head high, ears pricked, then she whinnied, and set off after them at a canter. Her action was good, free and true, and she carried her head and tail high. Alison wondered if she went as well with a rider. She watched them for a few minutes as they slowed to a walk, and began to graze again, before she whistled the dogs, who were chasing happily about. Then she walked back, ploughing through the rough purple heather to the stables.

Colin was crossing the yard with two full water buckets when she arrived. There was no sign of Christine.

"Been for a walk?" asked Colin, putting the buckets down and opening Jack's door.

"I went to have a look at some heath ponies," replied Alison.

She told her cousin about them while he straightened Jack's sheet, which, as usual, had slipped, and then asked where Christine was.

"Getting breakfast," replied Colin. "Though I don't know what she's going to get. There's not much left."

"I suppose we shall have to go shopping then," said Alison gloomily. She did not want to spend a moment away from the stables.

"Yes, and ring the hospital again, and see how Miss Blythe is," replied Colin. "They didn't tell us much last night."

"Well, she had only just had the operation, so they didn't know much, I suppose," said Alison.

"No." Colin closed Jack's door. "Look, you water the ponies, and I'll finish these and start mucking out."

Alison went off, and after giving Puck and Melody a drink she began to muck them out.

There was only Albatross left to be done when Christine shouted, "Breakfast."

They dashed in, to find that Christine had discovered three more eggs, toasted the last half loaf, and found a quarter of a packet of cereal. The milk had already come, but there was no tea or coffee, and so they had a glass of milk each. There was no butter or sugar left, and only about a quarter of a jar of marmalade.

"One of us must go to the village to-day," said Christine firmly, looking at the table. "There are only two tins of vegetable soup, a tin of ham, and a jar of pears left."

"That would do for lunch," replied Alison, eating her egg rapidly. "We needn't go until this afternoon."

"What! Without any bread, or potatoes or anything?" asked Colin. "And no sugar or butter?"

"You needn't go anyway," said Christine, who knew that the argument to persuade her cousin to go shopping would not be worth the results, as Alison was sure to forget everything.

"Oh, good!" Alison had expected the job to fall to her. "I want to try some of the ponies."

"Oh, no you don't." Colin could see himself being left with the grooming. "There's plenty of work yet."

"Don't be miserable," said Alison turning her egg upside down and pushing the spoon through the shell. "We shan't have to work all the time."

Christine was about to say something when there was a bang on the back door, and on going to investigate Alison found the papers. She carried them back, and they spread them over the table. A magazine on horses was mixed up with the daily papers. Alison grabbed the magazine and was soon immersed. Colin took one paper and began to read the cartoon page while Christine started on the other.

At last Alison, having looked at all the photographs, read an article on Combined Training events, and looked at the advertisements, dropped the magazine, sprang to her feet, startling the dogs, who jumped out of her way, and opened the door.

"Come on," she urged. "We've got to finish mucking out, water again, feed them, bed down, and groom."

Colin looked up from the latest film revues, and agreed that he supposed they should get on.

"I'll wash up," said Christine drearily. "But as soon as you've fed them, and mucked Albatross out, come in and help. The beds and grooming will have to wait until we've arranged the day's work."

"What about rides? Are there any?" asked Alison.

"The book is in the tack room," replied Christine.

Alison dashed off to fetch it. A few minutes later she was back, carrying the thick diary which Miss Blythe used to book the riders.

"There are some. I didn't really read them though," she announced, dropping the book on to the table with a thud that shook the crockery.

Christine picked it up, and found the day's date. On the page was written:—

11.0 a.m. Anna Field.
           Mrs. Pollitzer.
3.0 p.m. John Trevor. Jumping lesson.
Collect horse from station 1.30 p.m.

"We're going to be busy," said Colin. "And there's all the house work, and the shopping, and where on earth are we going to put another horse?"

"Well, let's arrange the jobs first," suggested Christine, beginning to collect the plates. "I'll wash up and make the beds while you finish mucking out, and I suppose you had better groom something for the eleven o'clock ride. But in future you must make your own beds, and help wash up."

"Who's taking the ride?" asked Alison suspiciously.

"I don't know," answered Christine. "It's really Colin's turn."

"What about me?" asked Alison indignantly.

"You look too young," replied Christine. "The riders wouldn't think you were safe."

"I like that. I can take a ride as well as you," retorted Alison. "I used to take some of Captain Right's."

"Yes, but the riders won't know that," replied Christine soothingly. "You can ride this afternoon sometime."

Alison agreed rather doubtfully.

"We can't very well decide what to give them until they arrive," said Christine. "We don't want to repeat yesterday's performance."

"Mrs. Pollitzer might be able to ride Trix though," replied Colin. "And Anna could have Melody, and I could have Puck. He's strong enough, and I don't see what else she can ride, unless we try to catch something."

"What about fetching the horse from the station?" asked Christine. "Who can do that? Do you think it's Stone Crossing, or Midgely?"

"Goodness knows," replied Colin. "We had better telephone them, and see if they are expecting a horse."

Christine agreed and Colin went off to 'phone. Alison went out to start the work, leaving Christine to clear away and begin the washing up. Colin rang Stone first, and was told that no horse was expected that day. Midgely said yes, they had a horse arriving for the Stone Heath Riding School that day on the one-thirty train from Yorkshire.

Colin reported this to Christine, and they decided that she should fetch it, leaving Colin and Alison to do the midday work and get ready for the jumping lesson.

"And we don't even know which pony jumps," said Christine, drying plates rapidly.

Colin went out to help Alison. They bedded down, and put a bed down in one of the empty stalls for the new horse.

"What about Albatross's walking exercise?" asked Christine, at half-past ten, when they collected in the tack room. She had finished the washing up, made the beds, and tidied up everywhere. She was now wandering round with a piece of paper and a pencil, trying to make a shopping list. She had also telephoned the hospital, where they had told her that Miss Blythe was doing well, but was rather worried about her horses. Christine assured the voice that the horses were very well, and that Mr. Davidson was helping them, and rang off after being told that they would soon be able to visit Miss Blythe.

Outside, everything was done except for some of the grooming.

"Alison can take Albatross out," said Christine. "I'll go to the village and do the shopping. It's a good thing Mummy gave us plenty of money."

They brushed over the two ponies, and at ten to eleven Alison, who was fetching Trix's tack from the tack room, met Mrs. Pollitzer on the doorstep. She was a smallish, grey-haired woman dressed in old jodhpurs and a blue shirt. She looked, in spite of her hair, very young, though when Alison had more time to study her she realised that it was her very bright, dark eyes, small, alive face, and slim figure that gave the impression of youth. She greeted Alison with a broad smile.

"You'll be Alison Dalby," she said. "Edna told me you were coming to stay with her. How is she?"

Alison explained, and Mrs. Pollitzer looked horrified.

"She said that she hadn't felt too well lately, but I'd no idea that there was anything really wrong," she said. "I must go and see her. Are you managing all right?"

Alison told her about Christine's adventure the day before, and she laughed.

"So poor Christine had to ride Jack," she said. "Why, even the Major has a job with him sometimes."

"Is he very good?" asked Alison.

"What, haven't you ever heard of Major Davidson?" asked Mrs. Pollitzer. "He used to jump for England. He had two horses. Silver Dawn and Roland. Wonderful horses. It was a dream to watch them. Dawn was always my favourite, though Roland was a big, bold jumper. Dawn was a beautiful little grey horse. She would jump anything. You never felt it was high enough because she always looked as though she could go higher. I remember her at the White City one year, only just over fifteen hands, jumping off against Norman Ware and Mosaic. He was over seventeen hands, a huge, ugly animal. Dawn won. There were five jump offs. I always remember her leading the canter round. She looked like a pony against him, or a show hack, with her perfect action. But she broke a leg out hunting a year later, and had to be shot."

"How awful," exclaimed Alison. "She did sound lovely."

"She was," agreed Mrs. Pollitzer. "But come, it's nearly eleven o'clock. We must be keeping the ride waiting. Shall I saddle Trix?"

She saw Alison's doubtful expression, and laughed.

"It's all right, I used to own her," she said. "I gave her to Edna when I had to go out to Australia three years ago."

"Oh, that's all right then." Alison handed her the chestnut's tack. "We were wondering what to do about mounts."

Mrs. Pollitzer went off to saddle Trix, and Alison took down Melody's tack. Christine was saddling Puck, and Colin was trying to get the stains off Trix's white socks.

They had just finished saddling up when Anna Field arrived. She was a tall, dark girl of about fifteen. She wore her long, shining, brown hair in two plaits, and was neatly dressed in well-cut jodhpurs and jacket, a black jockey cap, and new jodhpur boots. She said that she had only ridden a few times, and always on Puck or Melody. She was on the lead on Puck, but not on Melody.

"That's all right, you're riding Melody," Colin told her.

When she and Mrs. Pollitzer were mounted, Colin got on to little Puck himself, and Mrs. Pollitzer led the way through the gates and down the path, saying that she knew a suitable ride.

Melody walked out well, her ears flickering backwards and forwards, listening to her rider and watching the horse ahead. She was the perfect beginner's pony, quiet, but not a slug, willing, but not too sensitive for jerky, awkward aids.

Puck, full of his own importance as usual, bounced along with his little chestnut ears so pricked that the tips almost met. His thick crest with the bristly, hogged mane, was arched, his one blue eye and one brown eye shining. In the lead walked Trix, her fine tail carried high, her lovely head up and her long mane flowing over her hard, rich chestnut neck. Mrs. Pollitzer sat very quietly, with a loose rein.

They crossed the road into the birch woods, and broke into a steady trot down the sandy ride. Trix still led. Behind her Puck bounced happily, Colin having to hold him back firmly to prevent his barging into Trix's quarters. Melody trotted beside him, perfectly quiet, ignoring the excited little chestnut pony beside her. Anna was riding quite well, with naturally light hands.

They reached the end of the woods, and Mrs. Pollitzer led the way down one of the many rides across the heath.

Chapter Four

TOREADOR

BACK at the stables Alison had taken Albatross out, and Christine collected the dogs, and set out for the village. She found that it was very small, with only three shops, a general store and post office, a butcher's, and a wool shop.

It took her rather a long time to do the shopping as she was stopped by almost everyone she met and asked for the full story of their arrival, and about Miss Blythe's illness. But at last she had all the items on her list, so she walked back to the stables. To her surprise there was someone in the kitchen, a small, plump, middle aged woman.

"I'm Mrs. Rogers," she told Christine. "Miss Blythe asked me to keep an eye on you, and look after the house while she's away. I'm sorry I couldn't get here any earlier. How have you been managing?"

"Perfectly, thank you," replied Christine. "I've just been shopping, and the others are riding."

"It's a good thing you know something about horses," Mrs. Rogers told her. "I'd not have known what to do with them."

She unpacked Christine's shopping, and began to

put it away. Christine helped her, and they had just finished, when they heard hooves in the yard, and the ride returned, accompanied by Alison on Albatross. Christine dashed out to take Melody, and Colin reported a successful ride.

They put the horses away, and fed them. Then Christine glanced at her watch, and gave a gasp of dismay.

"It's ten to one!" she exclaimed. "And the horse is arriving at half past. I must go."

She tore into the house, grabbed her riding coat off a chair, and asked Mrs. Rogers if she knew when there was a bus. She was told that there was one in five minutes. She dashed into the tack room, grabbed a spare snaffle off its hook in case the horse had no bridle, and ran down the path to the bus stop. She was just in time. The bus came into sight, and a few moments later she was on her way to Midgely.

The journey took half an hour. She got out at the station and rushed on to the platform, only to be told that the train was running fifteen minutes late.

She wandered round the station, talked to some cows in a pen, who were waiting for a train, played with the station cat, bought some chocolate at a shop just outside the station, and arrived back on the platform just as the train came in sight.

When it stood hissing and panting in the station Christine ran down to the end of the platform, where she could see a horse box. As she opened the door of the

The horse stood on the far side

passenger compartment, and climbed in, she heard thumps and snorts from inside. Dimly through the hatch she made out the dark shape of a horse's head. He was standing in a corner, having travelled loose. All she could see was that he was a dark colour, and had a white mark on his forehead.

A porter arrived, and told her that the box would be pushed into a siding. The box was uncoupled, and two porters proceeded to push it back down the line, and off into the siding, until it stopped at a weed smothered unloading platform, with a cattle pen built on it. Christine had discovered the horse's tack, a battered old cavalry saddle, a curb bridle with a rusty bit and mildewed leather, and an old blanket which was obviously used under the saddle.

The porter opened the top doors of the box, and helped Christine climb up. They were in the shadow of an engine shed, and the inside of the box was rather dark. The horse stood on the far side, and still she could see only his dark shape, and thick neck.

She approached him very quietly, and slipped the reins round his neck. He allowed her to bridle him, and then the porter let the ramp down, and she led him out. Now she could see him properly for the first time. He was a strongly built little stallion, seal brown in colour, with a strongly muscled neck and quarters, good shoulders, long mane and tail, and slightly Roman nosed head. He was one of the showiest horses that Christine had ever seen.

She handed the reins to a porter, and the horse stood fairly still while she saddled him. He was about fifteen two she supposed, and very powerful. She hoped that she would be able to control him.

She led him out of the station, accompanied by the porter, who said he had a cob of his own that went in a trap, or followed hounds as well as anything else on the Heath. He held the stallion while Christine mounted in the station yard. The horse did not like standing whilst she adjusted her stirrups and tightened the girth, and when the porter let him go he sprang forward excitedly. He felt very bouncy, as she rode down the slope from the station, and entered the main road. He shied at cars, pedestrians and bicycles, jogged, and went sideways. He carried his head with his nose pressed right into his chest, which Christine found rather strange. He was terribly overbent, and he lifted his knees very high, almost like a hackney. If she loosened the reins he snatched at the bit, hesitated, and seemed surprised, so she kept them short, with a strong feel on his mouth which he seemed to like, as he settled down a little and began to walk more calmly.

They reached the outskirts of Midgely, and Christine remembered that it was a fairly straight road. Reaching a grass verge, she took him on to it, and told him to trot. He moved off at a fast, hackney trot, his nose again brought right in to his chest, so that all she could see was the arch of his neck, ending in two little, pricking ears. He snorted with excitement as he went, and kept a steady pull on the reins. She tried to bring him back into a slower trot, and then told him to canter. He started off into an extremely slow, almost standing, canter, his nose, if possible, even further in, his feet striking out in front of him at every stride. Christine pushed him on, and he extended a little. Then, finding a smooth stretch of verge in front of her, she pushed him to a gallop. She was astonished at the power under her, and, afraid that she might not be able to stop him, she started to bring him back to a trot, a feat which took some time and strength, as he seemed to have no real mouth at all, and was excited by the short gallop. But as soon as she had him walking he quietened down, and they continued quietly on towards Stone Heath.

At the stables Alison, Colin, and Mrs. Rogers had finished lunch, leaving some for Christine. Alison and Colin were helping with the washing up, and discussing the jumping lesson.

"Mrs. Pollitzer said that Puck is quite a good jumper," said Colin. "I wonder if I ought to ride as well."

"No, I shouldn't think so," replied Alison. "Captain Right never did, when we had jumping lessons."

"It seems awful to try to teach someone to jump," said Colin. "We can't jump much ourselves."

"We ought to practise," replied Alison. "Let's

teach ourselves."

"We can't very well do that," replied Colin. "Not without Miss Blythe's permission."

"I'm sure she wouldn't mind," replied Alison. "As long as we don't use Melody, or let any of them hurt themselves."

"We probably should," replied Colin gloomily, drying forks without thinking what he was doing, and dropping one.

"Now it'll have to be washed again," Alison told him. "Why should we hurt them? We needn't use fixed jumps."

"No, I suppose not," agreed Colin.

"By the way, what about the two youngsters?" asked Alison. "Shall we start breaking them?"

"I shouldn't think so," replied Colin. "We should probably ruin them, and Miss Blythe would be furious. I wonder how Christine's getting on."

"All right, I expect," answered Alison, finishing the drying, and beginning to put things away. "I'll go and brush Puck over when I've finished this."

She finished in record time, dashed outside, seized a dandy brush from the tack room, and ran across the yard to the shed. It was a glorious day, hot and still, with a deep blue sky and blazing sun. The dogs were stretched out in the sun in the jumping paddock, and Colin wandered out there to put up a small course of jumps. He wondered how good John Trevor was. Not too good, he hoped.

He was just fixing a single pole at two feet when Punch and Prunes woke up, and raced barking across the yard. Colin followed, and saw Christine coming down the path on a dancing, overbent, seal-brown horse, with a very long mane, who was throwing his forefeet about, and watching the barking dogs with sharply pricked ears and suspicious eyes.

Colin ran across to the gate and swung it open, calling to Alison. The stallion danced through, and Alison rushed out of the shed, tripped over the step and gave a cry of surprise.

"Help, what's that?" she asked.

"Our new horse," answered Christine, stopping the stallion, and dismounting. "He'll have to have a box."

"Whose?" asked Colin. "Albatross needs a box because he's been lame. Jack must have a box because he's a livery, and he'd probably kick a stall to pieces anyway."

"Trix will have to move," replied Christine. "We can't possibly put this animal in a stall."

"But . . ." began Alison.

"She's right," Colin interrupted her. "After all, it won't hurt Trix to stand in a stall."

"Poor Trix," said Alison. "She will hate a stall."

Colin handed her the mare's halter rope, and she led her away.

"I'll put a bit more straw down in there," Colin told Christine.

He dashed off to fetch it, and Christine waited until it had been shaken down before leading the stallion in and unsaddling him. He roamed round the box, snorting and scraping up the straw, then he had a long drink of water and hung over his door, staring round the yard, with water dripping off his whiskers, and his ears very pricked. He squealed at Jack, and Albatross came to his door and looked out to see what was happening. The stallion screamed again, and raced round his box.

"I hope he won't try to jump out," said Christine nervously, watching him.

They were all startled when a voice behind them said, "I say, what a lovely horse."

They turned to find a boy of about eleven, with red hair and freckles, standing watching the stallion dash round.

"I'm John Trevor," he told them. "I'm having a jumping lesson at three o'clock, or I was, but Miss Blythe's ill, isn't she?"

"Yes," replied Christine. "But we'll try to give you one if you like. We won't guarantee it will be marvellous, because we aren't very good ourselves."

"Fair enough. I just wanted some practice before the show," replied John.

"Show?" asked the Scotts and Alison, who had returned, together.

"Yes, the Heath show," replied John, sounding surprised. "It's in a month, at Midgely. They have it every year. It's mostly classes for Heath ponies, with some jumping and gymkhana events. They have dozens of other animals as well, and a fair and circus and everything."

"What are you riding? Puck?" asked Christine.

"Yes," answered John. "I always ride him. I jump him, take him in the showing classes, and gymkhana him. He's jolly good. We were second in the bending last year, and reserve in the showing. But we had three refusals in the jumping. That's why I want to practise. Miss Blythe will hate missing it. She was going to enter Red Morning in the class for Heath ponies that have been backed this year."

"Who's Red Morning?" asked Colin.

"The chestnut colt," replied John. "He's on the Heath now. Miss Blythe was taking everything she'd got this year, she won a lot with them there last year. She's already entered them, and Dolly and her foal are going. And the grey. She was going in one of the shown in hand classes. Elsie Downs was entering, and Major Davidson, but Miss Blythe doesn't take a lot of riders there—not like the other shows we go to. Just one or two. It would have been fun. Now, I suppose, I shall take Puck, and Major Davidson will jump Jack."

Christine, Colin, and Alison looked at each other.

"Why shouldn't we?" asked Colin. "We ought to be able to manage."

"We should be able to, but the question is, could

we?" asked Christine.

"Don't be such a wet blanket," shrieked Alison. "Of course we could do it."

"How far has Miss Blythe got with Red Morning and the grey?" asked Christine.

"She was lunging Morning without a rider, and the filly leads quite well in a halter, but she has got to wear a bridle for the show," explained John.

"We could try," said Christine. "I don't see that we should do any harm."

"I shouldn't think we would," replied Colin. "After all, we watched Captain Right when he was breaking in Daydream."

"But we've never tried it ourselves," said Christine.

"But think what a waste of entry money it will be if they don't go, after Miss Blythe had paid the fees," cried Alison.

"Anyway, we ought to get on with John's lesson," Christine changed the subject.

John fetched Puck from the shed, and they all went out to the paddock.

"Can Trix jump?" Alison asked John suddenly.

"Yes. Miss Blythe has entered her for the local jumping at the show," replied John.

"Do let's try her." Alison turned to her cousins.

"Well, I suppose it wouldn't hurt, not over these," replied Christine. "I suppose you'll want to ride her?"

"Of course," agreed Alison.

"All right then," Christine turned back to watch
John.

Alison dashed off, and was back in almost record
time with Trix. She mounted, and rode the mare round
the paddock outside the jumps once or twice to get the

feel of her. Puck went round for the second time, and
the Scotts corrected what faults they saw.

Then Alison turned Trix towards the first jump, a
brush, about eighteen inches high. The chestnut bounded

forward, and flew over, hardly seeming to bother to jump, and went on towards the next jump, a two-foot wall, which she jumped rather big. Alison got slightly left behind, and let the reins run through her fingers to avoid touching the mare's mouth. Trix went at the third jump flat out, with her head in the air, and before Alison had time to shorten her reins she had galloped past the jump, and was charging across the field. Alison hurriedly shortened her reins, and managed to pull up on the far side of the field. She rode back to the jump, and this time Trix jumped it perfectly, and went on over the other two low jumps. Alison cantered her back to the others, finishing with a triumphant buck as she came round the corner.

"She jumps all right," admitted Christine. "But we had better not take her to the show."

"Why not?" asked Alison. "She'll be perfectly all right when she gets used to me."

"And when you get used to her," replied Colin.

"I suppose if Miss Blythe agrees you could try," said Christine. "And Albatross should be ready by then. Is there a hunter class?"

"Yes, Miss Blythe's already entered him, and she was going to start trotting him again before she was ill," replied John.

"We shall have to arrange who is to ride what, and bring in the heath ponies for some schooling, and grooming," said Christine, in rapidly growing excitement.

"Do you think Miss Blythe will let us do it?" asked Colin.

"I should think so," replied Alison. "Why not?"

"Dozens of reasons," replied Colin. "We might ruin them, or let them get loose on the roads, or let them fall over the jumps, and spoil their mouths, and disgrace the Stone Heath Riding School."

"Don't be so pessimistic," cried Alison. "If we really work, we shall be perfectly all right. We must go."

"How do we catch the heath ponies?" asked Christine. "We can't just walk up to them as though they were in a field."

"We can to Golden Chord," said Alison.

"They have to be driven in," offered John. "That is how Miss Blythe catches them."

"But there won't be enough of us, will there?" asked Colin.

"Not really," agreed John. "Miss Blythe usually has about four other people with her."

"Well, we're supposed to be going to see her to-morrow, and so we can ask her all about it then," said Christine.

"And if she says we can go to the show, then we can start thinking about getting the ponies in," said Colin. "We ought to get on with your lesson now, John."

And so they turned their attention back to the jumping paddock. John took Puck round the jumps again, having raised them to about three feet, and Alison followed with Trix, who had settled down, and was jumping more calmly.

Then Alison took her in, and John schooled Puck round the paddock, and jumped him again. When the lesson was over John took Puck in himself, and then helped them to settle the rest of the ponies for the night. The stallion was a lot calmer, and when they left him he was pulling contentedly at a full hay net. They had decided not to give him a short feed until they knew what he was supposed to have. John went home and Mrs. Rogers had supper ready in the house. They had missed tea completely, preferring to eat a large supper at about seven o'clock.

Mrs. Rogers went home for the night, after they had assured her that they would be quite safe, and she had written down her address and 'phone number, as, luckily, she lived in one of the few houses in Stone that owned a telephone.

After she had gone they sat about in the comfortable lounge, with the windows wide open to let in the cooler evening air, which smelt of the heath, heather, and the sea. The sun was low, but it was still hot, though cooler than it had been during the day. They discussed the next day's arrangements, and examined the daybook, in which was written,

11.00 a.m. Roberta Graham.
Jeanette Boxer.
"I suppose it's your turn to go with them, isn't it?"

Colin asked Christine.

"I wish I could take one," said Alison.

"You can, when people know us better," Christine promised her. "But we'd be sure to get someone saying you were too young at present."

"I suppose so," agreed Alison.

"We can go and see Miss Blythe in the evening," went on Christine. "We shall have plenty of time. The visiting hours are six till seven, and we should have finished here by five."

The others agreed, and Alison said, "I do hope she'll let us go to the show."

"I should think she'll let us take some of them anyway," said Christine. "Even if she doesn't want us to take the youngsters, or jump Trix."

Alison was about to reply when the telephone rang. Colin went to answer it, and a voice at the other end said, "It's Shaun O'Rorke speaking. I wanted to inquire about my horse. Did he arrive safely?"

"Oh, you must own the stallion," said Colin. "Yes, he's quite all right." He went on to explain about Miss Blythe.

"Oh, I see. I'm sorry to hear it," came the reply. "I'll be over to see my horse to-morrow morning. His name is Toreador."

"What feed do you want him to have?" asked Colin.

"Oh, about four pounds of oats a day," replied his owner. "No more, he gets too fresh on many."

"All right, we'll remember," promised Colin.

"I'll see you to-morrow then," said Shaun O'Rorke. "Good-bye." He rang off, and Colin put the receiver down.

"Who was it?" asked Christine.

"The stallion's owner," replied Colin. "He says he's coming over to see it to-morrow. Its name is Toreador."

"What's the owner's name?" asked Alison.

"Shaun O'Rorke," replied Colin.

"Sounds Irish," remarked Christine.

"It certainly couldn't sound much more so," agreed Colin.

"We shall have to groom Toreador well in the morning," remarked Alison. "His owner won't be pleased if he looks as dirty as he did when he arrived."

"It was only dust and dried sweat," replied Christine.

"You shouldn't have brought him home so fast," her brother told her.

"I didn't. He sweated in the train," retorted Christine.

"Thank goodness Mrs. Rogers arrived," said Alison. "We should never have had time to do all the work in the house as well as the stables."

They sat up, discussing the show, until eleven o'clock, when, after a last look round the quiet, moonlit yard, they went to bed.

Chapter Five

PLANS FOR THE SHOW

A LISON woke up early again the next morning, and sprang out of bed to look at the weather. The sun was shining, the sky was blue, and there was a faint, hazy mist. It all promised another scorching day.

Alison shook Christine hard, dressed as fast as she could, hurled her bed together, and dashed downstairs noisily and out through the kitchen, forgetting to wash or clean her teeth, and waking Colin, who was not very pleased, as it was only half past six.

The dogs raced out after her, as she went across to the sheds, and said good morning to Trix, who was pleased with the apple which Alison had brought her, and seemed none the worse for being in a stall.

Toreador squealed excitedly when he saw her, and banged on his door with a forefoot, exciting Jack, who ran round his box, and kicked the door. Albatross looked out mildly to see what all the fuss was about, and then Colin arrived in the yard, asking if Alison had to sound like an elephant so early in the morning, and wanting to know what was the matter with the horses.

Alison explained, and Colin wandered across to look at Toreador. Then Christine appeared, and they decided to get the mucking out done. They set to work, and by seven-thirty the horses were all mucked out, and the day beds were put down. At eight o'clock Mrs. Rogers arrived, and got breakfast ready whilst they fed the horses.

After breakfast they groomed, Colin doing Toreador, who disliked being groomed, and laid back his ears, swished his tail, and waved his feet about. Christine did Jack, and Alison spent ages on Trix.

They took about an hour over these three, and then gave the rest a shorter grooming. There was no sign of Shaun O'Rorke when eleven o'clock arrived, and Roberta and Jeanette arrived for their ride.

Christine rode Trix, and the two girls had Puck and Melody. They went a ride which Roberta knew, and got back just after the hour, as Colin and Alison began their lunch. The ride had been successful, and the girls booked for the following week.

They were in the middle of lunch when they heard a car coming down the rough path from the road, and a few moments later it swung into the yard, and came past the kitchen window. It was a small, green sports car, driven by a red haired man. It swung round, narrowly missing the corner of the tack room, and stopped. The engine was switched off, and the driver got out and walked across to the boxes. He glanced at Jack, and Albatross, and then came to Toreador, who was at the end of the row. Seeing the horse inside the box, he opened the door, and went in.

66

"That must be Mr. O'Rorke," said Colin. "I had better go and see him."

He went out, and the other two saw him cross the yard to the stallion's box, and speak to the man inside. They talked for a few minutes, and then Colin came back across the yard accompanied by the stallion's owner, with Punch and Prunes jumping up at them and barking.

Arriving at the door Colin introduced Shaun O'Rorke, and turned to Mrs. Rogers.

"Will it be all right if Mr. O'Rorke has lunch with us?" he asked.

"Yes, and welcome. There's plenty," agreed Mrs. Rogers.

The stallion's owner thanked them, and came right into the kitchen. He was a medium sized, slim man of about twenty-five, with untidy red hair, brilliant blue eyes, and a tanned skin. He grinned at them all, and sat down in the place that Mrs. Rogers showed him.

"Did you think Toreador looks as though he travelled well?" asked Christine, after a short pause.

"Yes, very well," was the reply, with a trace of an Irish accent. "He's not looking at all tucked up. You'll be the one that rode him home. And how was he behaving himself?"

"Very well," replied Christine.

She described her ride from Midgely.

"He's a good horse," she was told. "Unless he gets one of his bucking fits."

"Does he buck a lot then?" asked Alison.

"Not so much, but he can when he's a mind to," replied Shaun.

"Can he jump?" asked Alison next.

"He can. If it wasn't for his being a bit excitable, he'd be the best jumper in the country," replied his owner.

"Have you had him long?" asked Colin.

"No, not very long," replied Shaun. "About two months. I got him at a sale. Some film company that had been up north filming were selling off their horses. He was one of them. They'd brought him over from Spain, where he used to be used in the bull ring. There was nobody interested in him at the sale. They were all after hunters, or riding-school types, and he was going begging, so I got him for twenty-five pounds."

"He seems to have quite a history," remarked Christine.

"Yes, he has," agreed Shaun. "And I hope he'll make himself a bit more in show jumping, if only he quietens down."

"Shall you ride him this afternoon?" asked Alison.

"I was thinking of it," answered Shaun.

"Do you live in Stone Crossing?" asked Christine.

"No, Midgely," replied Shaun.

He finished eating, and after helping Mrs. Rogers to clear away and wash up they wandered out. There were no more rides until three-thirty, when two people were coming for an hour's hack. Colin was to take them.

Alison was supposed to be taking Albatross out, but she waited to see Shaun start first. The stallion sidled about the yard whilst he adjusted his stirrups and tightened the girth, and then Shaun rode him through the gate into the paddock. Toreador squealed and shook his head when he felt the grass under his feet, and Shaun tried to make him walk properly, but the stallion jogged and sidled, and finally Shaun said, "I'll let him have a gallop."

"I thought he wanted it to calm down," said Christine, as Toreador shot off with his head between his knees, Shaun urging him on, and letting the reins hang on his neck.

The stallion shot round a corner on the wrong leg, almost fell, did a flying change with his forelegs, became disunited, bucked, got himself on the right leg, bucked again, and changed back to the wrong leg. Shaun seemed quite unmoved by the bucks, and he made no attempt to steady the horse. He was leaning forward, one hand resting on his horse's neck, ready to grab the thick mane. He was not bothering to keep any feel on the horse's mouth, and he did not seem to notice that they were on the wrong leg.

They went round about five times, each lap faster than the last, until at last Shaun tightened the reins, and began to slow Toreador up. The brown horse did not want to stop, his blood was up, and he wanted to go on and on. But Shaun insisted. The stallion squealed angrily, and made a dive forward. Shaun pulled him sharply back to a canter, and Toreador lost his temper. His head vanished between his knees, his back arched, and he threw himself into the air. Shaun tried to pull his head up, but without success. The horse landed with all four legs stiff, and went into the air again, leaping as high as he could, and twisting sideways in the air. Shaun was still there when he landed, and the stallion went into a furious series of bucks, throwing himself about the paddock like an unbroken bronco. He spun round, squealing and grunting as his hooves hit the ground with a jar that Colin and Christine felt from their place by the fence. Alison shot out of Albatross's box to see what was happening.

Shaun's grip was rapidly loosening, and as Toreador gave a particularly strong buck he lost it altogether, and flew over the stallion's head. Toreador, having succeeded in getting rid of his rider, took off round the paddock again, kicking up his heels, and sending lumps of mud and turf high into the air. Shaun picked himself up, and glared at the galloping horse.

"Does he often do that?" asked Christine faintly, wondering how she had stayed on him all the way home from Midgely.

"Oh, no. Only when he gets excited," replied Shaun, watching Toreador drop back into a trot.

"How are we supposed to catch him?" asked Colin, visions of spending the night chasing Toreador round the paddock looming up before his eyes.

"He'll come when he calms down a bit," replied his owner.

The stallion was walking now, his nose trailing along the ground, trying to snatch mouthfuls of grass and watch his master at the same time.

"Come on boy," urged Shaun, edging towards him.

Toreador gave up all pretence of eating and shot away at a gallop again. Having gained the temporary safety of the far end of the field, he began to graze in earnest, still with one eye on his would-be captors. When Shaun was only a yard away from him he swung his quarters round, and threatened to kick. Shaun dodged, and the stallion trotted away, head high, reins trailing. Again they followed him to the end of the paddock. This time he watched as they approached, spread out in a line, in an attempt to corner him, but he left dodging a moment too long. Shaun had his reins, and he was caught.

Instantly, he was all friendliness. He nuzzled his master, obviously remarking that he would never dream of bucking him off, and then stood like a rock for Shaun to mount. This time he condescended to walk, trot and canter fairly quietly round the paddock on either rein. Then Shaun announced that he was going to jump. The jumps were all at about three feet, after John's lesson the day before.

As soon as Toreador saw them in front of him he wanted to gallop. He was furious when Shaun would not let him, and he started to buck again. This time, however, Shaun managed to keep his head up, and he decided to take off instead. He went straight for the first jump at a flat out gallop, cleared it by a foot, and jumped the rest in the same way. Then he started another bucking fit and again Shaun came off, though this time he kept hold of the reins. After a few experimental attempts at getting free, Toreador stood still, and allowed his owner to remount.

Again they tried the jumps, and this time the stallion jumped slightly more steadily, and Shaun managed to stay on.

"Can you put them up?" he shouted to the Scotts.

They obliged, and again Toreador jumped clear.

"Let's give him one really good one to finish off," suggested Shaun, trying to dissuade the stallion from hurdling the gate and charging off through the yard.

Colin and Alison raised the gate to the five-foot peg, and the rest of the jumps to between four feet three and four feet nine. Shaun turned the stallion towards them, and he plunged forward eagerly. They jumped another perfect round, the brown horse seeming hardly to notice the height. They finished with a buck, and Toreador galloped round the field before Shaun could stop him.

"Well, he can certainly jump," said Colin, as Shaun rode back to them. "But does he have to do a rodeo act as well?"

"Oh, it makes it more interesting," replied Shaun seriously.

"Do you mean you enjoy those bucks?" asked Christine.

"Of course. Why do you think I keep him if I didn't?" asked Shaun in surprise.

"But can't you teach him not to?" asked Alison.

"Why?" inquired Shaun. "I should hate to ride a slug."

Alison could not think of an answer, and they went back to the stables leaving Shaun walking Toreador round the field to cool him off. He was still doing it when Colin's riders arrived, and Alison went out on Albatross.

That evening they set out on the ten minutes past five bus for Midgely. They had finished as early as they could, and were determined to be on time at the hospital.

"Now, what shall we tell her?" asked Christine, as they rocked along the rather rough Heath road.

"Oh, about Toreador, and the rides, and that we want to go to the show, and about Mrs. Rogers, but not about Christine riding Jack, or Shaun being such a mad rider," replied Colin.

"Why not?" asked Alison. "It's his neck, and his horse, not Miss Blythe's."

"All the same, I don't think that sort of news would exactly help persuade her to agree about our going to the show, or stop her worrying," replied Colin.

"Oh, I do hope she'll let us go," cried Alison.

They reached Midgely at last, and the helpful conductor told them how to reach the hospital. It was a big, modern, red brick building, which would have been nice if it had not looked so new. It had a garden all round it, which blazed with rather orderly beds of flowers. It had plenty of large windows, and when they had pushed through the swing doors they found themselves in a large, light hall, with the reception desk in the centre, and stairs, lifts, and passages leading off in all directions. It was not quite six o'clock, and there were several people standing or sitting about, obviously waiting

74

until it was time for the visiting hour to begin.

Christine was informed that Miss Blythe was in ward eight, on the first floor. They wandered round the hall, reading the notices on a board, and wondering where all the corridors led to, until a nurse appeared and told everyone that they could go into the wards.

The children dashed up the nearest staircase, and found themselves on the first floor. They stopped, wondering which way to go, until Alison spotted a nurse in a small room just across the corridor, and asked the way. She was told to go right, turn left at the first passage, and she would see ward eight in front of her.

They followed these directions, and found themselves standing outside the door of ward eight. They all hesitated for a moment on the doorstep, and then Christine said, "Well, what are we waiting for?" and they trooped in.

They had not seen Miss Blythe for two years, but they recognised her at once, three beds down from the door. It was a pleasant ward, containing eight beds, with large windows overlooking the gardens. The three children made their way across the ward to Miss Blythe's bed. Alison skidded on the polished floor, grabbed the corner of the sister's desk in the centre of the ward, and sent a blotter and ink stand clattering to the ground. With face aflame, she picked them up, dropped them back on to the desk, much to the amusement of the patients, apologised to the grim looking sister, and fled

75

after the others in a complete panic.

Miss Blythe greeted them with a cheerful smile, and started to apologise for being ill at such a bad time. She was about thirty-five, with short, curly black hair, dark eyes, and a weather tanned complexion. Even now she had plenty of colour, and she said that she felt much better.

When they had told her all the news, leaving out Shaun's mad ride and Christine's attempt to ride Jack, Alison asked the question that had been in all of their minds.

"Do you think—I mean—please may we go to the Heath show?" she asked, and added, "With all the horses that you were going to take."

"Except for the youngsters, anyway, if you think we might make a mess of them," added Colin.

For a moment Miss Blythe said nothing. Then she said, "I don't see why you shouldn't. Major Davidson will be going, and he's sure to keep an eye on you, and Mary Pollitzer is certain to go. If you're careful with them, I don't see why you shouldn't take the youngsters as well. I wanted to take them rather particularly, as it would be a good advertisement for me, and I might get some more to school. You must be careful with them though, and if you do find yourselves getting into difficulties, leave it until you can get Major Davidson, Mary, or me to help you."

"Oh, thank you. We'll be terribly careful, and we'll

do our best to win something!" cried Alison. "Isn't it marvellous" she went on, turning to her cousins. "I can hardly wait to start."

"There is no need to feel that you have got to win something," Miss Blythe told them. "As long as you enjoy yourselves, and don't break your necks or the horses', I shall be quite happy."

"It's awfully good of you to let us go, Miss Blythe," said Christine. "We really will be careful."

"I'm sure you will," replied Miss Blythe. "And for goodness sake call me Edna. I hate being Miss Blythe."

"What about catching the young ones?" asked Colin.

"You'll have to drive them in," replied Edna. "But don't try until you can get Mary or Major Davidson to help you, and don't pester the Major, he's very busy at the moment."

"What shall we ride?" asked Christine. "Will it hurt Melody?"

"No, not if you take her carefully," replied Edna. "You shouldn't have to gallop about too much, and she isn't that bad. Only a bit weak in front, and it wouldn't do her any good to be ridden a lot by heavy people, or jumped very high. Once you get them moving towards the stables they should go steadily enough. It would be different if it were one of the big round ups, with dozens of foals, and completely wild ponies. You may have a bit of trouble with the two youngsters, but I think you'll find that they will follow the rest, if they are all together to start with. They usually are."

"Yes, I saw them the other morning," Alison told her. "There were two others as well."

"Oh, were there. Well, drive them in with the rest, and then let them go when you've caught the others," Edna told them. "You can't keep all the ponies in until after the show. You'll have to turn Red Morning, Storm Cloud, and Dolly and her foal out again, but you can keep Golden Chord and Oberon in. There's a field at the farm down the road where you can turn them out. It costs more than the heath, but it's useful when I leave the ones I'm using out, as I usually do, if there's no show or anything coming. Teach the foal to lead, or he may be difficult at the show."

"Will Mrs. Pollitzer want to ride Trix herself?" asked Alison anxiously.

"Mary? No, she doesn't like riding in shows," replied Edna. She grinned at Alison. "I suppose you want to?"

"Yes, I should love to," replied Alison.

"Well, good luck. Try to keep her steady, and don't let her get her head down when you finish the course," replied Edna.

"Then I can jump her?" asked Alison joyfully.

"Yes, of course. I saw you all ride when I came to stay with your mother, Christine, and none of you struck me as being quite incompetent." She was openly laughing at them now. "You didn't think I'd be quite such an ogre as to tell you that you weren't to go?" she asked.

"Well . . ." began Alison.

"You thought I wouldn't like you to go without me to keep an eye on you," Edna finished for her. "If it wasn't for Mary and the Major I should be doubtful, but they can keep an eye on you quite as well as I could. Besides, it's a month off yet. I ought to be able to be present myself by then, although I shan't be able to ride, of course."

Then a buzzer rang somewhere, and Edna said, "That'll be the end of visiting hour. Good luck, and don't forget to keep Trix steady Alison."

"I won't," promised Alison.

"Thank you very much. We'll come again as soon as we possibly can," said Christine.

"You can't come tomorrow," Edna told them. "You have a five o'clock ride. Sheila and Norman Price. They're only beginners. They ride Puck and Melody."

Then sister arrived, and reminded them that visiting hour was over. They said good-bye to Edna, and hurried out. They caught the bus at twenty minutes past six and discussed the show the whole way home.

"It will be fun," said Alison for the twentieth time. "Just think. I can jump Trix."

"Who'll lead Storm, and who'll show Morning?" asked Christine. "And what about Dolly and her foal, and do you think Shaun will want to jump Toreador? I wonder which class Major Davidson will put Jack in."

"The open, I should think, if there is one," replied Colin. "We must get a schedule, and find out for sure which classes they are entered in."

"There must be one somewhere at the stables," said Alison. "Miss Blythe—I mean Edna—must have had one."

"I suppose so," agreed Colin. "Unless it's got lost, or chewed up, or something."

"Mrs. Pollitzer or the Major will probably have one anyway," said Christine. "And we can always send for another one."

They arrived back at the stables to find Jack's box empty, and his tack missing. The Major's car was in the yard, and both dogs had gone.

"They must have followed him," remarked Colin, when they had called for a few minutes without result.

"I hope they'll be all right, and not get kicked, or run over," said Alison rather anxiously.

"Punch would have more sense, and Prunes must be used to horses by now," replied Christine.

They found that Mrs. Rogers had gone, leaving them a cold supper in the pantry. They watered the horses, and just as they were finishing they heard hooves on the track, and Major Davidson rode into the yard on Jack, with the dogs at his heels. He rode across to them, and dismounted. They described their hospital visit to him while he unsaddled his horse, and Colin helped him to rub down the big bay. He agreed to keep an eye on them at the show, and to give them a hand with the youngsters when he had time. Then he said, "I'm free to-morrow afternoon. Would you be able to get them in then, or have you a ride? The sooner we get them started, the better."

"That would be marvellous," Christine assured him.

"What about the Prices though?" asked Colin.

"Who?" asked the Major.

"A ride, at five o'clock," replied Colin.

"Oh, those Prices," said the Major. "That's all right. They don't do more than trot a bit. You can take them in the paddock. It won't hurt the ponies."

"Oh, good! Then we can really get the ponies in to-morrow," cried Alison. "What shall we all ride?"

"You take Melody, you're the lightest," replied Christine. "Colin, Puck, and me, Trix."

"And I shall have Jack," finished the Major. "Though he'll probably go crazy when we start."

"What time shall we begin?" asked Colin.

"Two o'clock suit you?" asked the Major. "Then we can let them rest for a bit before the ride."

"Yes, lovely," agreed Christine. "How shall we find them?"

"Oh, they aren't far away," replied the Major. "I saw them when I was out. They're about a mile away, on the other side of that copse."

He waved his riding cane in the direction of a small wood not far from the stables. "They won't move far

81

before to-morrow."

They thanked him again, and then, after a final look at Jack, he left, calling, "See you to-morrow then," as the car swung out of the gate.

"He is helpful, isn't he?" said Alison, as they wandered in for supper. "A lot of people wouldn't want to spend their time messing about with someone else's riding school ponies when they were as good as he is."

"I suppose he's so interested in horses that he doesn't mind what he's doing, as long as it's with horses," replied Colin. "But I do hope we shan't make a mess of things when everyone is being so helpful."

Chapter Six

IN TRAINING

THE next morning they got through the work as quickly as they could, and Alison rode Albatross down to the farm to ask if they might use the field. Having received permission, she rode Albatross back, giving him a few short trots wherever she found some grass, as Edna had said that he should start work again now. He was going quite sound, but they were to take him very gently, and keep on with the embrocation, to make certain that he recovered properly.

The grey hunter was a comfortable ride, with a long, free stride, a good head carriage, and a nice mouth. He was always interested in everything round him, but he never shied, although he had hardly had any work for the last month or so. Alison thought how much she would like to hunt him, but then she remembered Trix's bouncy gaits, and excited plunges, and decided that she would prefer to hunt her.

They had lunch early, and saddled up, and just before two o'clock the Major's car swung into the yard. He parked it in the usual place, and fetched Jack, who was ready saddled and bridled. The children fetched their mounts, and they rode out of the yard, leaving the dogs shut in Jack's box, as they would only be a nuisance. Elsie and Harry were there to shut the gate once the ponies were through, and then they sat on the gate to wait.

The Major led the way towards the copse where he had seen the ponies the day before, and sure enough they were still there, grazing on the other side of the trees, still accompanied by the bay, her foal, and the brown.

The red chestnut youngster saw them first, and raised his head to watch them. The others followed suit, and the whole herd watched warily as the four riders spread out. They rode round until they were behind, and on either side of the little bunch, and yet still too far away to alarm them. But the grey youngster had scented danger, and swung round in an attempt to break away.

The Major raised his hand, the signal to close in, and they broke into a fast canter. He had hoped to get them started more quietly, but if the grey got away then the rest would follow.

The Major turned the grey back, and she dashed off towards the copse. Red Morning tried to swing out to the side, but Christine drove him back. Trix knew what to do, and though she was terribly excited she did whatever Christine told her, and added her own bits when she realised that Christine was not sure what to do. Puck and Melody also knew their job, having been on round ups, and having been rounded up themselves many times. Jack, on the other hand, had never done anything like this before, and he was almost unmanageable. He bucked and plunged, grabbing at the bit, and almost getting away from his rider. Oberon tried to get past him, but the Major managed to turn Jack into the brown pony's path, just in time, swinging the lash of his hunting crop in the pony's way. They all carried crops with lashes, and Christine kept getting hopelessly tied up in hers as Trix was turning and twisting after the ponies so fast and so skilfully that Christine was almost shot off. But at last they were crossing the Heath towards the stables, with Oberon and Red Morning leading. Dolly was used to this sort of thing, and she refused to hurry herself, although her foal was terrified. But seeing how calm his mother was, he stopped trying to race away ahead of her, and stopped close to her side.

Elsie and Harry had the gate open, and were keeping out of the way until the ponies were in. Oberon knew the way, having been driven in dozens of times, and he had slowed to a pace that was sometimes a trot and sometimes a canter. Jack, though much quieter, still wanted to race, and he was pulling. Trix was black with sweat, though she still watched the lolloping herd with both eyes and both ears in case one should try to get away. Puck and Melody puffed along at the back, still keeping a watchful eye on the herd. The strange bay and her foal, and the brown were still there, the brown challenging Oberon's lead now, and making the pace faster for a moment. But the stables lay just ahead, gate wide, and Elsie and Harry standing quite still at a little distance. Oberon made a last minute attempt to escape, but Trix was there before him, and Jack was closing in on the other side. Too late, Oberon found escape impossible, and he shot through the gate with an angry toss of his head, kicked up his heels, and galloped across the yard to the field gate. The four riders dismounted outside it, loosened their mounts' girths, panting for breath.

"Very successful," said the Major. "And now, we have only to catch them, and let the strangers out."

Elsie, Harry, and Alison held the horses, leading them round to cool them off, and Christine, Colin, and the Major climbed the gate into the yard, collected halters from the tack room, and a bucket of oats from the shed, and set to work catching the ponies they wanted.

Golden Chord and Dolly came easily, and Oberon followed after slight hesitation. Storm Cloud was a little more difficult, but they cornered her between the end of the boxes and the paddock gate. Red Morning was the worst. He dodged behind the other two loose horses, and charged about the yard, refusing to be cornered, and kicking at them when they tried to grab him. But at last they managed to herd him into a corner by the road gate, and the Major got a halter on him. Once caught, he became tractable, and allowed himself to be led into the shed, and tied up in the stall next to Storm.

As the gate was opened, the bay and the brown shot through, and galloped out of range. Then they stopped, and turned to watch. The bay whinnied, and Storm

He charged about the yard

answered with a high, babyish squeal. Toreador, who had been going crazy inside his tightly closed box whilst the ponies milled round the yard, screamed a reply, and raced round the box, while Albatross gave his deep, calm whinny. Christine opened Jack's door, and both dogs threw themselves on her in a frenzy of delight. The Major took Jack and led him across to his box. They put their ponies away, leaving Puck and Melody's tack in the shed near them, and then they discussed taking the ponies down to the farm.

"Red Morning, Storm, and Dolly will have to go down," said the Major. "Dolly's foal will follow her, and the youngsters should lead all right."

"Edna said that Storm doesn't lead very well yet," remarked Colin helpfully.

"Well, it will be a lesson for her then," the Major told him. "If you lead her, Alison can take Red Morning, and I'll take Dolly. It will be good practice for you as well. Christine had better stay here and wait for the Prices. It's half past four now, and we may have trouble persuading these animals to lead."

They fetched the ponies, and the foal, who was still keeping as close to his mother's side as he could. The Major led the way with Dolly, Colin went second with Storm, and Alison brought up the rear with Red Morning. Christine watched them go, and then started filling water buckets and straightening beds.

The three pony leaders were getting on quite well.

Dolly walked calmly in the lead, her small dun foal pressing close to her flank, his eyes wide and startled. Storm led quietly at Colin's side, hesitating slightly from time to time, but going on again as soon as Dolly drew ahead. Morning led perfectly, keeping his nose just a little ahead of Alison. They were almost at the farm when Storm suddenly stopped dead, head high, an expression of horror on her face. The Major glanced round to see why she had stopped, and told Dolly to stop as well.

"She's seen a goat!" exclaimed Alison. "Look!"

Sure enough, there was a large white goat tethered on an open piece of ground beside the road. It was watching them with interest, and Storm stared at it with an expression of terror.

"I'll go on ahead," said the Major.

He led Dolly on, and Colin tried to persuade Storm to follow. She tried to run backwards as soon as he attempted to lead her on, and tried to swing round. Morning began to fidget, and paw the ground.

"Bring him on, past her," called the Major.

Alison obeyed, and the chestnut jogged nervously past, and shot after Dolly, almost pulling Alison over. Storm shot forward, nearly jerking the rope out of Colin's hands, swung half-round as she felt the jerk, stumbled, almost fell, recovered with a frightened snort, and dragged Colin past the goat, until she reached the other two, when she stood and shook, head high, looking back at the goat, and uttering piercing snorts. Colin patted her, and told

89

her that she was a silly girl, and they proceeded more steadily to the farm, leaving a rather puzzled goat staring after them.

When they had turned the ponies out, they started back to the stables, discussing the show as usual.

"It wouldn't be a bad idea to ask the farmer to tether a goat near the field," said the Major. "A lot of horses are afraid of goats and pigs, until they've got used to them."

"Do you think they'll be ready for the show?" asked Alison. "Do you know what we have to do in the 'Backed This Year' class?"

"Just ride round, with someone at the pony's head, then dismount, and each youngster gives a show in hand," explained the Major. "Morning should do well. He's well made, and his action is good."

They arrived back at the farm to find Christine's ride just ending. She was very interested in the goat episode, and said that the ride had been a success. She had let both children have a canter, and the ponies had behaved perfectly. Golden Chord and Oberon had been making rather a noise, and excited Toreador.

The children settled the horses for the night, and then Major Davidson left, and they wandered in to supper.

The next day the weather broke. They awoke to find the skies grey and stormy, and the rain blowing across the Heath in gusts, making it look bleak and cold. Jack kicked Alison when she was mucking him out, and

Prunes found Trix's tail bandage just after Christine had
finished rolling it, and trailed it round the yard, covering
it in mud, and tearing off one of the tapes.

They ate breakfast in miserable silence. They had
planned to give the youngsters a lesson, start teaching
the foal to lead, to take Golden Chord and Oberon in the
paddock for schooling, and give Trix and Puck a jumping
practice. There was a three o'clock ride, and Albatross
was supposed to go out for his hour of walking and
trotting. Also, the tack needed cleaning.

They finished the bedding down, and Christine was
annoyed to find Colin and Alison having a straw fight
in the sheds, spreading straw everywhere. They promised
to sweep up, so Christine went off to groom Jack.

She finished him, and wondered where the others
were. Going into the shed to see if they were there, she
found Alison grooming Trix industriously, with everything swept, and in perfect order. There was no sign of
Colin. Alison said that he had gone down to the field to
see that the youngsters were all right.

"Is he going to give Storm a lesson?" asked Christine.

Alison agreed that he was, and Christine muttered
something about grooming the rest of the horses first,
and went off to do Toreador.

Up at the farm Colin was having trouble with Storm.
He had caught her fairly easily, with the aid of a bucket of
oats, and put her halter on. He led her out into the lane
at the side of the field, and began to lead her along it

towards the village. She did not want to leave the other horses, and she dragged and dawdled. Colin began to think that perhaps it had not been such a good idea to

give the filly a lesson after all, but it was too late to turn back.

Storm went more and more slowly, looking back longingly towards her field, and whinnying. The rain ran down Colin's face, and his mackintosh was turning dark with water. The halter rope was wet and stiff, and water ran down the filly's mane and made dark lines down her hind quarters. She looked dirty and common, with her wet, muddy coat clinging closely to her flanks, her long, tangled tail straggling round her hocks, and her untidy mane lying unevenly on either side of her neck.

"Oh, come on horse," begged Colin, giving the halter a tug.

Storm decided that she had gone far enough. She dug her toes in, laid back her ears, and assumed a mulish expression.

"Come on, walk on," ordered Colin, turning his back on her, and attempting to lead her forward.

Nothing happened. Storm's head dropped lower,

and her ears went flatter.

Colin stepped back level with her shoulder, and tried to make her walk on. She stood quite still for a moment, then, as he continued to click at her, and tried to push or pull her forward, she took a step backwards.

"Storm, walk on," snapped Colin.

Storm took no notice. She had raised her head, and was staring at something farther down the road. Colin followed her gaze, and was horrified to see a large tractor approaching. Storm's head went higher. Her ears pointed further forward. Her nostrils were extended.

"Good girl," said Colin. "It's all right. Steady lady."

Storm tried to whip round, but Colin managed to hang on to her. The tractor stopped, panting and puffing out clouds of blue smoke.

"Come on then, good girl," said Colin.

Storm shivered, and tried to rear.

"Take her back down the road. There's a farm back there you can take her in," yelled the driver.

There was nothing for it but to give in. Colin let the shaking Storm turn round, and they started back towards the farm, the filly jogging and pulling, and the tractor rattling along a few hundred yards behind.

They reached the field gate, and Colin led Storm in. The tractor rumbled past. Colin stood and thought. If he tried to lead the filly up the road again, she was certain to be awkward, and he had no one to help him. On the other hand, if he left her in the field she might be worse the next time, but the weather was so awful. Colin unfastened the halter, and let Storm go. She tore away across the field, neighing to the others, who came cantering to meet her. Colin started for home.

He arrived at the stables to find Christine grooming Golden Chord, who was filthy, and Alison out on Albatross.

"How did she go?" asked Christine.

Colin explained.

"Oh well, at least she didn't hurt herself, I suppose," said Christine resignedly. "But I do hope she won't remember next time."

"So do I," agreed Colin.

He went off to water, and met Alison. She was unsaddling Albatross, whose grey coat was dark and wet, and whose legs were covered in mud.

"He does look a mess," remarked Colin.

"Yes, those rides are awful," replied Alison. "I do hope it hasn't hurt his leg."

She hung the saddle on the door, and the bridle on a hook on the wall and began to rub the grey down with clean straw.

After that was done, they fed the horses, and went in to lunch.

Chapter Seven

≋≋

A MAD RIDE

AFTER lunch they started on the tack. The rider had cancelled his lesson and the paddock was far too muddy to ride in, even if it had not been raining so hard. Colin suggested going out for a ride, but Christine said that it would make the tack horrible, and they would not get it right for ages.

They cleaned Jack's and Toreador's tack, and Alison did Trix's. Golden Chord's and Oberon's and the saddle which they intended to use on Morning had not been used since the last time that they had been cleaned, so they only needed wiping over with a damp cloth and soaping, but Puck's and Melody's were filthy, and Albatross's badly needed doing.

They were hard at work when they heard a car squelching up the wet track from the road.

"Who on earth can this be?" wondered Christine, dropping her sponge into the saddle soap tin, and going to the door. She saw Shaun's green car stop, then he got out, and came across to the tack room. His car was open, and he had thrown an old tarpaulin across the seats. He wore an ancient riding mack and no hat. Water dripped off him, and the children looked at him suspiciously as he came towards them.

"You aren't riding, are you?" asked Christine apprehensively.

"Yes," was the reply. "Oh, have you cleaned my tack? I'm sorry. I should have let you know."

"That's all right," Christine told him, her tone belying her words.

"I'll ride him bareback," said Shaun, in the voice of one who has had a wonderful idea.

"Don't be silly, we don't mind about the saddle," replied Christine.

"I do though," answered Shaun. "The leather will get so wet. I'll just use my bridle. I promise to clean it when I get back. Nothing could make it much worse, anyway. It's almost dropping to pieces."

"You can't . . ." began Christine, but Shaun had already collected his bridle and gone.

"I say, let's go too," cried Colin.

"What a marvellous idea," shrieked Alison, grabbing Trix's bridle.

Colin grabbed Puck's, and Christine started to argue. But the others had already gone. Christine hesitated for a moment, her excitement at the idea rapidly overriding her objections. Then she grabbed Goldie's bridle, and ran through the door and across the yard to the shed, seizing her mackintosh from where it hung on a hook on the tack room door.

Shaun already had Toreador out in the yard, and he

was about to mount. Alison and Colin were still bridling as Christine dashed in, her riding mack half on and half off, and shot into Goldie's stall.

Colin was ready first. He led Puck out of the shed into the yard, his mack unbuttoned, and the belt dragging on the ground. Alison was having a job to get Trix's bridle on, as the mare insisted on sticking her nose in the air, and clenching her teeth. Christine had finished, and was leading Goldie out while her cousin was still fastening the drop noseband.

In the yard she found Shaun welcoming the idea of company, and Puck waiting impatiently to start.

Christine finished putting on her mack, vaulted on to the chestnut mare's back, and turned to see Alison scramble on to the excited Trix from the paddock fence.

A moment later they clattered across the yard, and out on to the track, followed by Punch and Prunes, who had no intention of being left behind.

It was still raining hard, and the reins were already slippery by the time they reached the road. Shaun was in the lead, with Toreador bouncing excitedly. Shaun did not know the rides, but Christine promised to guide him.

As soon as he found himself on the sandy track in the birch woods Shaun gave the stallion his head, and was away at a flat-out gallop. Trix, almost mad with excitement, gave three bucks and followed, with Alison sitting on her neck. Puck and Goldie tore after the other two, Puck giving a few kicks in his usual style, and

Goldie catching up rapidly and then passing him.

Alison managed to wriggle back on to Trix's back, and collect her reins again. Then she looked up to see Toreador flying down the track ahead of her, Shaun just sitting there, not attempting to slow him. Behind she could hear Puck's and Goldie's hooves. Goldie was well ahead of Puck now, but both ponies were moving as fast as they could.

They reached the end of the wood, and Shaun went straight on along the sandy ride. The stallion's neck, for once in his life, was stretched out, his tail streaming behind him. Trix tore after him, Alison feeling rather unsafe on the slippery, smooth back, with her mack flying out behind her, and both leg straps broken.

Christine had discovered that though Goldie was comfortable, and did not buck, when she tried to suggest slowing down a little the pony completely ignored her.

Colin was trying to push Puck on even closer to Goldie. The fat little pony scuttled along as hard as he could with Colin leaning forward, trying to take his weight off the pony's back a little, and pricking his fingers on the hogged mane.

Alison, on the bouncing Trix, wished that she had not cleaned the mare's bridle quite so enthusiastically. The soap was beginning to lather, and the slippery leather felt horrible between her fingers.

Shaun was trying to pull Toreador up now, as they were approaching the end of the ride, where the farm lands began. The heath stretched away on either side of them and behind them, running for many miles, but this was the extreme end of one side.

Alison began to slow Trix with difficulty; Christine found that the now tiring Goldie was much easier to stop. Colin managed to bring Puck back to a trot, and Alison turned Trix round to stop her. Shaun had jumped the hedge and ditch, and was vanishing along the side of a corn field, still at a gallop.

"Well, shall we follow, or what?" asked Colin, trying to grip Puck's slippery wet sides, whilst the pony bounced, and tried to buck. Trix was dancing sideways, impatient to be off after Toreador.

"We can get through that gate," cried Alison. "It isn't locked."

Christine, who had the quietest pony, dismounted to open it as it was too heavy to open when mounted. The others filed through, and she closed it, before mounting Goldie, and following the others at a slow trot down the side of the corn.

Trix, however, refused to trot. She cantered impatiently sideways, almost bouncing Alison off. They reached the fence at the other end of the field, and looked round for a way out. Then Alison spotted Shaun, well out across the next field, which was an empty grass meadow. He was only cantering now, and as there did not seem to be a gate, they realised that he must have jumped the rails which divided the two fields.

"Well, I suppose we shall have to jump as well," said Alison, who was not nearly as reluctant as she sounded. "I'll go first."

"No, you'll have her down," shouted Christine, as Alison turned Trix's head towards the fence.

Alison either did not hear, or did not listen. Trix cleared the rails beautifully and, with Alison clinging to her mane, dashed away across the meadow in pursuit of Shaun.

"This is hopeless," said Christine. "Isn't it horrible weather?"

"Awful," agreed Colin. "These two can't jump that. We had better try to find a gate."

They rode round the end of the corn field, and found some slip rails, which had been wired, but which, after a few moments work, came down easily. They replaced them carefully, before mounting their ponies again, and letting them canter on slowly in the direction that Trix and Toreador had taken.

They did not have far to go. They reached the end of the field, and saw Shaun and Alison sitting on their horses in the middle of a muddy cart track, which led towards some rather tumbledown farm buildings. They were talking to a tall, lanky man in a mackintosh, who had a brown lurcher dog at his heels.

Colin and Christine went through the open gate, and trotted along the cart track towards them. As they drew nearer they could hear Shaun saying:

"Sure, and how were we to be knowing it was private, when the little people have made off with the notice?"

The man remarked that he would have thought it was obvious that a corn field was not a public bridle path, and then turned at the sound of the other ponies' hooves.

"And I suppose you also missed the notice by the gate?" he asked.

"We certainly didn't see one, but I'm sorry if we were trespassing," replied Colin. "We just followed Shaun. He was being run away with."

"Sure, and it was the little people had hold of my bridle," Shaun told the farmer. "And who am I to be arguing with them about the path I should be taking?"

"Well, if you really were out of control . . ." said the man slowly. "This land is private though, and we've got some very valuable cattle out here, so we don't like people wandering about because of gates and dogs. I'll show you the way to the road."

He led them along the cart track, with Shaun keeping up a running commentary on the land, the weather, and the little people, while the children tried not to laugh.

Toreador was still very excited. He was cantering on the spot, and bucking. Trix had calmed down, and she consented to walk.

They reached the road at last, and found the open heath facing them again. The farmer, who had recognised the horses, told them the way back to the stables without being asked, and then vanished back down the track, with the brown lurcher still close at his heels.

"You are an idiot Shaun," gasped Alison, when she could stop laughing. "That poor man hardly got a word in edgeways."

"I must remember that bit about the little people having hold of my bridle," remarked Colin. "It sounds much better than just being run away with."

"It's a good thing Trix didn't hit that fence," said Christine. "Miss Blythe would have been furious. She did jump well though."

"I know. It was lovely," agreed Alison.

"I wonder where the dogs are," said Colin. "I hope they aren't lost."

"Oh, they're probably waiting for us at home," answered Christine.

She turned to look behind them, to see if the dogs were in sight, and saw Alison's miserable face.

"What on earth's the matter?" she asked.

"I think she's going lame," replied Alison in a small voice.

"What? Oh no!" cried Christine. "Trot her on a bit."

Alison obeyed, and there was no doubt about it. Trix was definitely going lame on her off fore-leg.

"Oh, help!" groaned Christine. "Edna will be furious."

"See if she's picked up a stone," suggested Colin, stopping Puck, and turning round to watch.

Alison jumped off in sudden hope, but there was only soft mud in the mare's feet.

The three children looked at each other dumbly.

"How awful," exclaimed Colin. "We were idiots."

"Yes, I should never have let her go so mad," agreed Alison miserably.

"It's my fault for letting you go," said Christine.

"Do you think you could have stopped us?" asked Colin.

"I should never have had such a stupid idea," said Shaun, dismounting. "Let me have a look."

He handed his reins to Alison, and Trix stood still, unheld, while he ran his hand down her muddy foreleg. She picked up her foot obligingly, and he examined it more closely. Then he felt her tendons, her knee, and her shoulder. He did the same to her other foreleg. Finally he stood back and shook his head.

"I can't find anything," he told them. "Trot her on again, Alison."

Alison did so, but she was definitely lame.

"You'd better lead her home, and then we can have a better look when we've got some of the mud off," said Christine.

Alison nodded miserably, and they made their way slowly towards home. Prunes and Punch arrived suddenly, muddy and panting, a few minutes later. The party went on through the driving rain, the horses suddenly quiet, drooping their heads, and tucking in

their tails as the rain blew over them. Their riders bent
their heads, hunched their shoulders, and wished they
were home. Their wet mackintoshes flapped in the wind,
the wet reins were stiff between their fingers, all the soap
and suppleness washed out of them, and their hands were
covered in black grease and saddle soap.

They reached the stables at last, and began to rub
down their wet mounts with straw. It took ages, but at
last they were all comparatively dry, and the children and
Shaun could turn their attention to Trix's leg. Colin felt
it first, looking for heat, or swelling, and found nothing.
Then Shaun had another look. He picked up her foot
yet again, and suddenly gave an exclamation of surprise.

"What is it?" asked Alison eagerly, craning over his
shoulder, and getting in the light.

When she had got out of the way again Shaun said:
"I've found what's wrong."

"Well?" asked Christine nervously, expecting a
cracked bone, or a torn tendon.

"It's an over-reach," announced Shaun. "It's hardly
broken the skin at all, but it must be bruised rather badly
to make her go as lame as she did."

"Thank goodness that is all it is," gasped Christine.
"I thought at least she'd be lame for a month."

"She should be sound in a couple of days, shouldn't
she?" asked Alison joyfully.

"Yes," replied Colin. "By the way, how did you
miss it when you were drying her heels?"

"I er . . ." Alison stopped and blushed violently.

"You forgot," said Christine. "Oh well, at least we've found out what it is, even if Alison did forget to dry her horse's heels. I was expecting to have to break the news to Edna that Trix was lame for life, or something."

Shaun went off to clean his bridle, and the others joined him. By the time the bridles were finished, and the horses settled for the night, it was supper time. They invited Shaun in, and afterwards Christine fetched the schedule that the Major had given them, and the list of ponies and the classes for which they were entered. Then they settled down to divide the ponies between them, and see which were being used by riders.

They decided that Alison should jump Trix in the "Local Jumping" class for horses and riders within a fifteen mile radius, and show her in the "Hack" class. She was also to ride her in the gymkhana events, and in the "Best Rider Under Fifteen" class.

Christine would ride Albatross in the "Hunter" class, and Goldie in the "Heath Showing" class and the races. She would also ride Red Morning in the "Backed This Year" class, with Colin leading him.

Colin had Oberon for the "Heath Ponies Under Saddle"—the same class as Goldie—and the races. He was leading Storm in the "Two to Three Year Olds in Hand" class, and Dolly in the "Mare With Foal at Foot" class. Christine was leading the foal in that same class.

"I haven't got any 'In Hand' classes," said Alison.

"You've got a jumping class," replied Christine. "You and John are the only ones."

John had Puck for the whole show, and Elsie had Melody for most of the classes. Shaun announced that he was entering Toreador for the "Local" and "Novice" jumping.

"I suppose Major Davidson is going to enter Jack for the open jumping," said Alison, reading the schedule. "Oh good! They've got 'Musical Poles.' I love that."

"I suppose I had better not enter Toreador in any races," said Shaun reluctantly. "He'd probably go crazy."

"I'm sure he would," agreed Colin.

Chapter Eight

SEA BATHING

THE following day dawned grey, but it was not actually raining. There was a strong breeze blowing, and it was much cooler. The children decided that it would be a good opportunity to do some schooling. They had two riders at eleven o'clock, so it would have to be in the afternoon.

Alison took the morning ride, which went off successfully to her delight, and as soon as lunch was over they collected halters and set off for the farm, leaving Alison behind to sort out lunging rein, whip, and mouthing bit.

They caught the youngsters fairly easily, and Storm followed Morning back to the stables without any trouble. They found Alison still searching unsuccessfully for the mouthing bit. After they had put Morning and Storm in the shed, they helped her to search, and Christine finally found it in a drawer in the kitchen, mixed up with the shoe cleaning materials, floor polish, and soap powder.

They decided to start with Morning, and leave Storm standing in the stall wearing the mouthing bit. They put the lunging cavesson on the chestnut colt, took the stirrups off the saddle, before putting it on him, and clipped the lunging rein to the front ring of the cavesson. Christine picked up the lunging whip, and they took the colt into the paddock.

They had moved the jumps to one side, to give themselves more space, and Colin and Alison, perched on the fence, watched Christine trying to persuade Morning to walk round her in a circle. He started, walked for a few strides, then suddenly shied, and swung round.

Christine had to coil up the lunging rein, turn the colt round, and start again. As soon as he was told to walk on, Morning whipped round again. Christine repeated the performance of sorting him out.

"You're too far in advance of him," called a voice behind Colin and Alison. "Drop back a bit, and keep just behind him."

Colin and Alison looked round to find Mrs. Pollitzer watching with interest.

"Keep the whip just behind him," she went on. "Then you can touch him with it to drive him forward if he wants to turn round."

She climbed the fence, and Christine tried again. The next time Morning tried to turn round, Christine was ready for him, and managed to prevent it with a light touch of the long whip.

"Good," called Mrs. Pollitzer.

After Morning had walked round a few times Christine told him to trot. He started smoothly, but after a few strides he bucked, and broke into a canter.

"Stop him, and make him do it again," called Mrs. Pollitzer.

Christine obeyed, and this time Morning behaved perfectly.

"Does he canter?" she asked.

"Yes. Don't let him go too fast," ordered Mrs. Pollitzer.

Christine told the colt to canter, and this time he behaved perfectly.

When Morning had walked, trotted, and cantered equally on either rein Mrs. Pollitzer said, "Why don't you back him now? He's ready for it, and you could put Albatross in the shed for a bit, and use his box."

Christine agreed, and they all went up to the boxes. Colin moved Albatross, and they led the colt into the empty box. When the lunging rein had been removed they put a snaffle bridle on him and some stirrups, and Christine held him while Alison leaned across his saddle once or twice to let him feel her weight in the stirrup. Then she mounted very quietly, landing as gently as she could.

Morning stood quietly, except for a slight stiffening of his back, and a nervous flick of his ears. Christine gave him a handful of oats, and led him round the box. Then Alison dismounted carefully, and remounted from the other side.

They led the colt round the box again, and the lesson

was over. They unsaddled the chestnut, and Colin fetched
Storm, and they put a snaffle bridle on her, and a halter
over it. It was the first time that she had been led about in
a bridle, and when Colin told her to stop, by saying,
"Whoa!" and feeling the reins, she stopped so suddenly

that he almost tripped over. She threw up her head, and
tried to run back, but Colin told her to walk on, and
finding her mouth free, she obeyed.

However, she soon settled down, and led well.

When they had finished her lesson they put her back
in the stall and saddled Goldie, Oberon, and Puck.
Mrs. Pollitzer, who had been told about Trix, and had

taken it very calmly—merely saying that they must have been mad—said that she would ride Albatross, who had not yet been out.

Alison rode Puck, Christine took Goldie, and Colin had Oberon. Mrs. Pollitzer sat on Albatross in the middle of the field, and they had a mock "best rider" class.

Mrs. Pollitzer made them walk, trot, and canter round her on either rein, and corrected their faults and their ponies' faults. Then she called them into the centre, and made them each in turn canter a figure of eight, trotting a few steps in the middle to change legs, back four paces, dismount, and remount on the off side. She also made them jump a two-foot pole.

When they had all done so she told them their chief faults. Puck was over bent, and bounced instead of cantering properly. Goldie lacked impulsion—Christine was having to kick her to keep her going—and Oberon stuck his nose out, and trailed his hocks.

They schooled busily, with Mrs. Pollitzer giving advice in between exercising Albatross gently round the field. He could canter to-day, but he did not get excited, in spite of having been kept walking for so long.

Christine used her legs furiously, and Goldie did seem to be going with a little more impulsion, though Christine's legs felt as though they were dropping off. Colin, who was trying to get Oberon to drop his nose, flex his jaw, and bring his hocks under him, was having to use his legs almost as hard as Christine, and Oberon still insisted on sticking his nose out, though at times he seemed a little better.

Alison was riding Puck on a fairly long, loose rein, trying to get him to stretch his neck more, and stride out, instead of jiggling and bouncing. Mrs. Pollitzer watched with interest. They were all working hard, and she decided that the Stone Heath School would have no need to be ashamed of them at the show.

They schooled for about an hour, with short periods of letting their ponies go round on a loose rein to rest them, in between collected work. When Mrs. Pollitzer, who had taken Albatross in some time before, finally called to them that it was time to come in, all the ponies were going much better.

They took the youngsters down to the field, accompanied by Mrs. Pollitzer, to give the foal a leading lesson. Colin stayed behind at the stables to start watering, and shake up the beds.

The foal was very nervous at first, but when he saw that Dolly took it all as a matter of course he began to follow her on the end of the halter rope. They rubbed his neck and back, getting him used to the feel of human hands on him, and then let him go. He raced round the paddock, kicking and bucking, getting his ridiculously long legs tied into knots, and giving shrill squeals.

They arrived back at the stables to find Shaun riding his stallion in the paddock, for once under control, and

Colin filling the hay nets. They had intended to catch the ten minutes past five bus into Midgely to see Edna, but when Shaun heard that they were going he offered to give them a lift in his car. They accepted gladly, for it was already five o'clock, and they did not see how they would be able to catch the bus anyway, as they still had to feed the horses.

They finished the work, and Shaun put Toreador in and settled him. Mrs. Pollitzer, who had been to see Edna the day before, had gone home. The children hastily changed out of their riding clothes, brushed the straw and hay out of their hair, and crammed into Shaun's little four-seater. They shot out of the yard, missing the gate by a fraction, and tore down the sandy track to the road.

Shaun was rather a wild driver, and they held their breath as he skidded round corners, avoided other traffic by inches, and narrowly missed hitting an ice cream cart. They were all rather glad when they reached the hospital alive.

Shaun left them on the steps, saying that he would be over to take Toreador out early the next day. Then he sent the little car leaping forward, and roared away, missing a van by a fraction, and swinging out of sight round a corner. They went on up the steps into the hospital.

*   *   *

The same roar woke Alison the next morning.

Looking at the old blue alarm clock, she saw that it was only six o'clock. Christine was sitting up in bed, sleepily demanding to know who it was, and downstairs the dogs were barking.

Alison went across to the window, and hung out. Shaun looked up, saw her, and waved cheerfully.

"I'll take him straight out," he called. "I shan't be long."

He went into the tack room, and reappeared with Toreador's bridle. He was about to enter the stallion's box when he had an idea, and turned again.

"Why don't you all come?" he asked. "I'm going down to the beach, to give him a swim."

"What a marvellous idea," shrieked Alison, almost falling out of the window in excitement. "We'd love to come, wouldn't we?" she added to Christine, who had joined her.

"I suppose so," agreed Christine, remembering previous ideas of Shaun's.

She and Alison hastily scrambled into their bathing costumes, put coats on over them, sandals on their feet, and dashed downstairs, calling to Colin on the way.

"Which ponies shall we take?" asked Alison, as they opened the kitchen door.

"Goldie, Oberon, and Puck," replied Christine. "Trix is probably still a bit sore, and anyway, she'd get so excited."

They ran across the yard, collected bridles from the

tack room, and dashed on to get the ponies ready. Until now they had not had time to go down to the sea, and they did not know where the beach was, but Shaun assured them that he did.

Then Colin appeared, still looking half asleep, and Shaun led Toreador out. The children collected their ponies, and scrambled on, Alison on Puck, Christine on Goldie, and Colin on Oberon.

Shaun showed the way through the gate, and turned into a path which led away across the heath towards the distant blue gleam of the sea. The sun was already warm, and there was a thin mist in the hollows. Far above them a lark was singing, and some ponies grazing near the track lifted their heads to watch the riders as they broke into a canter along the narrow path.

Toreador led as usual, plunging and pulling. Puck was next, his thick, bristly crest arched, his little red ears pricked, as he tried frantically to overtake the stallion. Oberon was next, going in his usual steady manner, with his smooth, comfortable, stride. Goldie, lazy as usual, came last, her ears flopping and her fair mane lifting slightly in the light breeze.

It did not take them long to reach the end of the heath land, where the heather and the wiry grass joined the pale sand of the beach. The tide was half-way in, creaming over the silver sands, and breaking lazily, as though the day were already too hot to be energetic.

The riders threw off coats and shoes, leaving them

above the tide mark, and vaulted back on to their mounts. They rode down the beach until the first white ripple of foaming surf washed over their ponies' hooves. Toreador advanced with high, surprised steps, lifting his feet carefully over the small waves at the edge, and blowing loudly at them.

Puck tried to drink, and wrinkled up his nose in disgust at finding it salt. Oberon and Goldie walked into the sea side by side, seeming quite used to this odd performance.

Shaun urged Toreador farther out, and the water was soon washing round his flanks, and over his shoulders. The others followed, Puck and Oberon soon finding themselves out of their depths, and starting to swim lurchingly. Then Goldie was swimming and, finally, with a snort and a lurch, Toreador was out of his depth.

The water was very cold, as the sun had not yet had time to warm it, and the riders gasped as it washed over them. The ponies were enjoying it, plunging through the waves, and starting to swim again when the short, higher ridge gave way again to deeper water.

They did not stay in many minutes, but soon turned their horses' heads shorewards. Toreador landed first, forged through the shallower water to the dry sand, and came out with a buck and a squeal. Then he plunged his head down between his knees, grabbed the bit in his teeth, and was off along the hard, smooth sand at a smart gallop. The rest followed, Puck bucking excitedly, sending

117

sand flying, and almost sending Alison over his head.

The children all found it difficult to get any grip on their ponies' wet sides, and the wet leather slipped through their fingers. Toreador was a flying, dark shape against the silver beach, and Shaun was making no attempt to stop him. Puck scuttled after him, smothering Oberon and Goldie in sand from his flying hooves.

Christine got a mouthful of wet sand, and Colin was blinded by it. They hung on to their ponies' manes, and forgot everything except the speed, and the flying sand and water. The beach ran for miles, unbroken and shining under the sun, and edged by the purple and brown heath. Alison began to wonder if Shaun would ever stop, but at last the stallion's pace slowed, and as Puck came level he dropped into a trot. Puck skidded to a standstill beside him, and Alison fell along his neck. Goldie and Oberon came up at a more sober pace, Christine and Colin having regained some control. They sat and panted for a few moments, and then turned the horses, and rode slowly back to collect their coats and shoes.

They got back to the stables at about half past seven. The ponies' coats were sticky with salt and sweat, and their tails were full of sand. The bridles had dried stiff and salt-caked, and everyone realised that they would have to be cleaned.

The children put the ponies away, brushed some of the stickiness out of their coats, and brushed out their tails as best they could. Then Shaun had to leave, roaring out of the yard in his usual mad style, and the others started to muck out. After the early swim they felt hot and uncomfortable in slacks. The straw seemed to creep down their necks, and hay seeds smothered their hair and got into their shoes, pricking their feet.

They were all glad when Mrs. Rogers called them in for breakfast, and as they ate they decided to leave the youngsters' schooling until the cool of the evening, and spend the morning washing the tails of the ponies who had been in the sea, and cleaning tack in the shade.

Unluckily the day did not work out at all like that. First they found that there were two rides, one at eleven o'clock, and one at three. Then Alison discovered that Puck had lost a shoe, so she had to set out for the nearest forge, which was in Stone Crossing, near the station. Colin took the eleven o'clock ride, and Christine saddled Albatross, and took him in the paddock for an hour. Edna had said that he could be given more or less ordinary work now, so she took him round at all paces, and pretended to be showing him.

That afternoon they were just starting to clean tack when the telephone rang, and Major Davidson said that he would be over at four o'clock. They had not had time to groom Jack properly that day, so Alison dashed off to do it. Then Christine took the three o'clock ride out, and Alison trotted Trix up and down the yard. She was going sound again, much to Alison's joy. Meanwhile, Colin got on with the tack while Alison started the

119

The bay jumped a very good round

tiresome job of washing the salt out of Puck's tail.

That evening they collected halters, and went down to the field to fetch the youngsters for another lesson. Alison gave the foal a leading lesson, and then ran back to watch Christine ride Red Morning. Colin led him round the yard with her sitting on him, with the reins loose, and her legs still. Morning seemed to be taking it all very calmly, and Christine said that she thought they could start teaching him the aids next day.

The Major had arrived at four, and had taken Jack in the paddock. The bay had been very fresh, but after a time he had settled down, and had finished by jumping a very good round with all the jumps on or over four feet. It was an experience just to watch their polished perform-ance, and Alison, sitting on the gate, and imagining Trix tearing round with her nose in the air, wondered if she could ever be as good in a hundred years.

Chapter Nine

※

THE STORM

THE days flew past, never seeming long enough for everything that had to be done if the Stone Heath Riding School horses were to be ready for the show on the first Saturday in September. Red Morning was soon going very well, and could be ridden about freely without being led. Storm Cloud was now very good to lead, and would pick up her feet to be examined, and stand still while she was looked at from every angle, had her legs felt and was groomed. They began to lunge her, and both she and Morning were led over to Stone Crossing to be shod. They were both very good, as they had had their feet tapped and filed and washed ever since they had first started to be handled.

Dolly's foal, Broken Biscuits, so called because he was developing darker flecks on his dun coat, making him look as though crumbs had been dropped on him, was also growing easy to lead and handle. Trix was going more steadily, Toreador still bucked Shaun off at regular intervals, and Puck was still as bouncy as ever, though he and John got on well together.

Elsie was practising hard with Melody in preparation for the "Best Rider" class, and Albatross was really sound again. The Major was giving Jack several jumping practices a week, taking him for a great deal of walking exercise, and riding him up and down every hill in reach, as well as going for ordinary hacks, and schooling him on the flat. Goldie's laziness was fast disappearing as she grew fitter, and lost her grass fat.

At last, much to everyone's delight, Edna came home from hospital feeling quite fit, but with a warning from her doctor that she must not attempt any strenuous work for several weeks to come.

Two days before the show, they decided to finish schooling, and go for a long hack to prevent the ponies from growing bored. It was a hot, thundery day, with a haze over the sea, and no breeze at all. The sun had a burning heat, and the weather forecast had hinted at probable thunder that night, but Christine thought that they would be back before the storm broke. Shaun had the day off, as he often seemed to have, and he was riding his stallion. Elsie Downs and John Trevor went too.

Christine rode Albatross, Alison rode Trix, Elsie had Goldie, Colin took Oberon, and John rode Puck. They did not take Melody, as they thought it might make her legs bad for the show. Edna warned them not to get too far from shelter, in case the storm came up suddenly.

They set off across the heath in the direction of the sea. The ponies went lazily, even Toreador and Trix, and their riders sat with loose reins, looking round at the countryside, and trying to spot the wild ponies. They carried their lunch with them, and intended to have it near the sea, when they found somewhere with both good grazing and some shade.

It did not take them long to reach the sea, and they turned to ride by the side of it, on the hard sand. The sea was completely calm, and rolled slowly and lazily up the beach.

They saw several groups of ponies, standing head to tail wherever there was a clump of trees, or a copse to shelter them from the burning sun. All the colour seemed

to have been burnt out of the heath, leaving it brown, with patches of dusty green. In the distance the heather-clad hills were purple and hazy, and the only things to break the monotonous colour scheme were the golden patches of gorse, blazing against the heather. Above, invisible in the intense blue of the hot summer sky, larks were singing.

They rode on for about two and a half hours, still by

the side of the sea, either on the silver beaches, or, where the sand changed to shingle, along the heather-covered sheep tracks. They stopped for lunch at about one o'clock, at the edge of a small birch wood, near which was a patch of fairly good grazing ground. They tied the ponies to trees by their halter ropes, being careful to tie Toreador a good way apart from the others, and then settled down to eat. In spite of the hot weather, they were hungry, as usual, and they ate most of the food, giving odd scraps to their ponies. Then they lay back in the heather and talked lazily, mostly about the show. At last Colin said:

"Well, we'd better move. We've a long way to go home, and we don't want to get caught if there's a storm."

"There won't be one yet," answered Alison calmly.

"Oh no?" Colin had stood up. "Then look at these clouds."

"What? Where?" The others scrambled to their feet, and followed Colin out of the shelter of the trees. The sky behind the wood was black, the sun, shining on the massed dark clouds, made them even blacker, and thunderheads floated ominously under them.

"We shall have to hurry!" exclaimed Colin, picking up Oberon's tack.

Alison grabbed Trix's, and the others, after one more look at the sky, hurriedly began to throw saddles on to their own horses. A light wind had sprung up, and the cloud bank was moving up fast, the first few wisps already drifting across the sun. Toreador, scenting the approaching storm, danced about madly as Shaun tried to mount, and Trix fidgeted nervously as Alison tightened her girths.

"Come on," said Christine, when they were all mounted. "Are your girths all right, Elsie?"

"Yes, I think so," replied Elsie, trying them again, and finding that they would go up another hole.

A few minutes later they were riding along the path towards home at a steady trot. Shaun led, as usual, with Trix bouncing along behind him.

"We had better go back the same way," said Christine, seeing that Shaun was looking for the short cut that he knew was in the vicinity. "If we get lost it will take much longer."

"I suppose so," agreed Shaun unwillingly.

The excited stallion broke into a slow canter, in spite of Shaun's attempts to keep him trotting, and Trix squealed, and bucked, almost sending Alison over her shapely ears.

The sun had disappeared by now, and it was obvious that the storm would break long before they got home. It had grown much cooler, and even Goldie and the sedate Albatross had woken up. There was an expectant, electric atmosphere in the air, as the sky grew darker, and the wind stronger. The sea was stirring now. The waves had white caps, and the surf was making more noise on the beach. They spotted a small group of ponies moving towards the shelter of some low gorse bushes.

The larks had stopped singing; they were silent and still.

They were still trotting, except for Toreador, who was pulling, and cantering every other stride. Then a sudden white flash made them jump, and the ponies shied. There was a short pause, followed by a long, low rumble. At the same moment the rain began to fall in slow, heavy drops, and the wind suddenly blew stronger, lifting the ponies' manes, and flinging spray from the tops of the waves.

They were still miles from home and the nearest shelter, having ignored Edna's warning, as the day had looked so fine.

"We're going to get jolly wet," remarked Christine helpfully, turning up her coat collar as the rain grew heavier.

"No!" said Colin sarcastically.

The sky was suddenly split by a long tongue of forked lightning, and the thunder was louder and nearer. Toreador plunged nervously, and the rest threw up their heads and started forward. Trix made a sudden dive, trying to get her head down, and almost got away from Alison, who hastily pulled her back to a trot.

"We shall have to let them walk for a bit," said Christine, a few minutes later. "We've been going for ages now."

They brought their ponies back to a walk, just as another fork of lightning seemed to hit the sea a few yards from the shore. This was followed immediately by a sharp, double crack of thunder which sent Toreador into one of his bucking fits, and made Trix shoot off at a gallop. She had covered some distance before Alison could pull her up, and by the time she had managed it Shaun had got the stallion's head up.

"What shall we do?" shouted Colin, patting Oberon, who was dancing nervously.

"Go on. There's no shelter worth taking in miles," replied Shaun, trying to keep the stallion walking.

The rain was coming down in sheets now, and the riders were feeling uncomfortably wet. Their saddles were rapidly turning grey in the deluge, and Alison, Colin and Christine all thought unhappily of the hours they had spent tack cleaning. Then a tremendous crash overhead sent Toreador crazy, and Trix began to buck. Puck gave three bucks, and sent John over his head, and Oberon and Albatross dived forward. Goldie did not turn a hair.

Alison was slipping farther and farther up Trix's neck, and Shaun seemed to have no control at all. The stallion's head was right down, and he was giving a bucking display in his best rodeo style.

John managed to keep hold of Puck's reins, and Alison gave up, and slid off over Trix's shoulder, although she hung on to the reins tightly as the mare tried to shoot off.

Shaun had lost both stirrups, and dropped his reins, which had slid down to Toreador's ears. The stallion twisted in mid-air, and Shaun flew off. Toreador stopped bucking, swung round on his hocks, and was off across the heath at a wild gallop. Shaun sat up and watched him go in disgust.

"Now we start trailing him for miles, I suppose," he remarked.

Another crash of thunder sent Trix up on her hind legs, and Alison almost let her go. John was still standing by Puck, while Christine, Colin, and Elsie sat on their ponies and wondered whether to chase the stallion, get off to help the others, or stay where they were.

Shaun collected a stirrup leather that had come off the stallion's saddle during his display.

"I suppose he'll break his reins, or lame himself," he said mournfully. "That will put an end to my going to the show."

They looked at each other through the blanket of rain, and wondered what to do next. John remounted, and Alison threw Trix's reins back over her ears, and started to mount, almost letting her go again as she whirled round in circles. In the end, Christine held Trix, and Alison managed to scramble on. When she was safely up Shaun said, "Well, it's no use you all staying, and drowning. I'll follow him, and you take the horses home."

"Don't be stupid!" said Christine. "Of course we'll help. Alison can take John and Elsie home, and Colin and I will stay."

"Why can't I stay, then one of you can take them

home?" asked Alison. "I'm sure to get lost."

"We can take ourselves back, or stay and help," offered John. "We both know the way."

"And wouldn't Edna be pleased!" said Shaun. "You must all go."

"Let's draw lots," suggested Christine. "Two of us will stay, but we must decide which two."

Elsie found a bus ticket in her pocket, and they tore it into strips, and drew for the shortest. Christine got it, and she rode off into the rain, followed by Elsie and John. Alison tried to stop Trix whinnying, and diving after them, and Colin and Shaun began to discuss plans of action.

"Though why three of us should get pneumonia chasing my horse, I don't know," said Shaun.

"Don't be silly, it's not cold," retorted Alison, who was hot from wrestling with Trix.

"Let's get started, anyway," said Colin. "We'd better separate."

"No, we should never find each other again," replied Alison. "Let's keep together until we see him."

"If we do!" replied Shaun gloomily.

They started off slowly through the driving rain, Trix dancing and sidling nervously, as the thunder rolled in the clouds. It was hard to see anything at all through the curtain of rain.

"How we shall ever find him in this I can't think," said Colin, peering through the curtain of rain.

"Nor can I," agreed Shaun.

131

They went on, stumbling through the deep heather.

"Look, you'll lame both those ponies if you go on like this," said Shaun at last, when Trix had caught her foot in some particularly deep heather, and almost fallen.

"Well, we can't go back now, we don't know the way," said Alison cheerfully.

"No, we don't," agreed Colin, in sudden alarm. "How on earth shall we get home when we catch Toreador?"

"Give the ponies their heads," replied Alison, patting Trix's soaked red neck.

"We could try that," agreed Colin dubiously. "But I doubt if it will work. Oberon would probably make for some haunt of his own, and Trix would probably dash off in the wrong direction."

"Why should she?" asked Alison angrily.

"Thunder," replied Colin, as another roll sent the chestnut mare waltzing sideways.

"Do you honestly think there's any chance of finding him in this?" asked Alison, after a short pause. "He might have gone home."

"Not he," replied Shaun. "He'll be roaming about somewhere."

"But where?" wondered Alison, who was growing cold now that Trix had calmed down a bit, and they were only walking.

"Now how should I know?" asked Shaun.

They went on in silence for a time, and then Colin

said, "It's clearing a bit."

"So it is," agreed Alison, staring up at the racing clouds. The rain was now only a thin drizzle, but the thunder still rolled in the clouds, though the lightning had died down to an occasional faint flicker. They could see farther across the heath, and they started to try and spot the stallion. But the only sign of life was a small, wet flock of sheep, and a distant band of ponies.

"Do you think he's over there?" asked Alison, trying to make out a saddled horse among the heath ponies.

"No, they're standing too quietly," replied Shaun. "If Toreador was there, they'd be moving about. Anyway, he's much bigger than any of those ponies."

"I suppose so," said Alison, and began to search the heath again.

They had been searching for an hour. The rain had stopped, and the clouds were dispersing. Soon the sky would be clear again. The ponies seemed tired, and all three searchers were wondering if they would find Toreador at all, and if so, would he be sound, and would he be able to go to the show? They were beginning to think of giving up, and going home to see if he had turned up, when Colin suddenly said, "What's that?"

"Where?" asked Alison and Shaun, looking wildly round them.

"There," Colin pointed across the heath towards a small gorse thicket.

"It's certainly a horse," agreed Shaun.

"I can't see anything," said Alison, trying to see a horse against the gold and green of the gorse.

"On the other side, I can see something dark," replied Colin.

"Oh yes!" Alison saw it as well. "It does look like a horse."

There was something that might have been a horse's back showing above the gorse. Then it moved, and a head and neck appeared at one end. The head wore a bridle, and when it saw them coming, it squealed.

"It's him all right," said Shaun.

The stallion came round the gorse into full view. He stood, head up, reins trailing, watching them as they came cautiously towards him.

"Can you catch him?" Alison asked.

"I might," replied Shaun. "You stay here."

Colin and Alison obediently stopped their ponies, and watched breathlessly as Shaun walked towards the motionless stallion. As he drew closer Toreador tossed his head, and half reared. Then he changed his mind, and took two tentative steps forward. Shaun stood still, and held out his hand. The stallion reached out his head as far as he could, and sniffed. Shaun kept still, holding a piece of bread out to his horse. Toreador shook his head, and shied sideways. Then he stopped again, his little ears almost touching at the tips, nostrils distended, as he tried to decide what to do. He was rather tired of wandering about the wet heath alone, and he had been unable to find any of the other ponies. Also, he was growing hungry, and he had found the coarse, salty grass unsatisfying, used as he was to oats and chaff and good hay, or meadow grass when he was turned out to graze.

He took another step forward, and he could almost reach the bread now. Another step, and he had it. As he reached out his head to take it, Shaun slowly slid his other hand up to the stallion's reins. The next moment Toreador was caught.

He shot backwards, and tried to pull away, but Shaun hung on, and Toreador gave in, and accepted a small carrot which Colin found in a pocket. Then Shaun fixed the loose stirrup back on to the saddle, knotted the broken reins, and mounted.

"At last," cried Alison, riding up on Trix. "Now we have to find the way home."

"It must be that way," said Colin, pointing vaguely across the heath.

"If we ride back to the sea, we can follow the shore until we come to the right path," said Shaun sensibly. "You can see Stone village from the beach."

"We can try," agreed Colin. "But it will take hours. Besides, where is the sea?"

"Over there," said Alison, pointing to where the sky looked brightest.

"Are you sure that isn't just the storm clearing?" asked Colin.

"Well . . ." Alison was silent.

All the copses and gorse clumps looked alike, and there were no tracks except the meandering sheep paths.

"Let's give the ponies their heads," said Colin. "It can't do any harm, and they may know the way."

"All right." Alison dropped her reins on to Trix's neck. Trix promptly began to rub her nose on her knee. When she had finished she started to graze. Alison pulled her head up, and used her legs, leaving the reins loose. Trix shot forward at a canter, and gave a buck. Alison lost a stirrup, and slid up her neck.

"Don't loose her, for goodness' sake," shouted Colin, as Alison pulled up, and found her stirrup.

Oberon was grazing, and Toreador was staring at the horizon with great interest, though there was nothing in sight except some sheep.

"Now what?" asked Alison.

"Try again, only don't kick her," suggested Shaun.

Alison loosened her reins, and Trix began to graze again.

"Let's start walking, and then give them their heads," suggested Alison.

"What direction shall we start in?" asked Colin.

"That doesn't matter," replied Alison, starting to ride along one of the narrow sheep tracks. The others followed. Alison gave Trix her head. For a few moments the mare went on in the same direction. Then, realising that she was free to go where she liked, she struck off at an angle through the heather. The other two followed.

Trix picked her way steadily and certainly through the gorse bushes and deep heather, and half an hour later they came over a rise, and saw the stables in front of them.

"Good old Trix," said Colin.

Alison patted her hard, and she broke into a jog.

They rode down the slope, and struck the path. Ten minutes later they were riding through the gate into the yard. Christine came flying out of the tack room to meet them, and began to ask questions. Alison explained as fast as she could, and Christine came to help her with Trix, and hear the rest of the story.

Chapter Ten

HARD WORK

WHEN they had settled the horses they took the three sets of tack into the tack room, and Christine, Elsie, and John began to clean it, while the others went in to get dry. Shaun had some dry clothes in his car. He said that as he got soaked so often he always had some with him. The others were soon out again, and hard at work. They did not use foot oil, as it was so near the show, but they soaped everything well. When they had finished, all the tack looked much better, though the saddle pommels, the front of the flaps and the head pieces, nosebands, and reins, were still rather grey.

"We can do it again to-morrow," said Alison, putting hers up on to the rack.

John and Elsie had to go, but Shaun helped feed and settle the horses for the night, then he dashed out of the gate in his car, narrowly missing the gate post, and Edna sent them all to bed early, as she knew that the next day would be chaotic.

They were up at six the next morning. It was a grey, windy day, and much cooler. They mucked out, bedded down and fed, and after breakfast they took the horses into the paddock for half an hour's quiet exercise. Shaun

138

was coming in the evening to exercise Toreador, and Major Davidson had been in very early to ride Jack.

When all the horses had had their exercise, the children started grooming, spending ages on each pony, and finishing by washing their tails and legs, and putting tail bandages on them. Then they fetched Dolly and Biscuit, and the youngsters up from the farm, and gave them a thorough grooming, before taking them back again, hoping that they might at least be a little easier the next morning, though Morning promptly found the muddiest patch in the field and rolled in it.

Then they started tack. It took ages, and they all began to wish that they had never thought of going to the show. Colin dropped the liquid metal polish, and had to go and fetch some more, leaving the girls still knee-deep in dirty tack.

About half an hour later Christine looked up.

"I wonder where Colin has got to?" she said.

"He is being ages," agreed Alison, finishing her third lot of tack which was Melody's, and hanging it up beside the other sets. Christine was just finishing putting Jack's bridle together, having cleaned it with great care.

"There are still three bridles, and all the head collars," Alison went on, looking round the tack room.

"And Dolly's bridle," added Christine, looking at the old snaffle.

"Oh, isn't tack horrible," sighed Alison, glaring at the bridle.

139

They worked on furiously for another twenty minutes or so, and then they heard a car turn into the yard.

"Shaun," said Alison, without looking up.

"Probably," agreed Christine, starting to clean Morning's girth.

Alison had started on the head collars, leaving Toreador's tack until after Shaun had ridden him.

Then Colin appeared in the doorway, looking rather sheepish, and put a fresh tin of polish on the edge of the saddle horse. He turned to find Christine and Alison looking at him rather coldly.

"In case you're interested, we've almost finished, except for the metal work," said Christine. "Where on earth have you been?"

"Down to the village," replied Colin.

"For an hour?" asked Christine.

"An hour. Oh help!" Colin looked even more sheepish.

"What were you doing?" asked Alison.

"I met Shaun," replied Colin.

"But he's got the car. He should have brought you back quickly," answered Christine.

"Yes, but he was trying to teach me to drive round a field, and it took rather a long time before I was any good at steering at all," explained Colin.

"Then you can jolly well clean Dolly's bridle, and help with the rest of these head collars. And then there will be Toreador's tack, when Shaun has finished with him," Alison told him firmly.

"He'll clean that," said Colin.

Shaun appeared in the doorway behind them, and agreed that he would.

"Oh, thank you," Christine suddenly felt much more cheerful. The thought of having to clean the stallion's tack later that evening, when everything else was finished, had been hanging over her. "I'll go and start watering."

She went off, and Alison and Colin finished the head collars, cleaned Dolly's bridle, and polished all the stirrup irons, and bits, with the new tin of polish.

In the end Shaun stayed to supper, as it was ready when he came in from the paddock. After supper Alison decided that her hair needed washing before the show, and she dragged Christine off to help her. Shaun and Colin went out to the tack room to do the stallion's tack.

When she had finished her cousin's hair, Christine decided to do her own. She had just started to dry it, sitting by her bedroom window, and watching Shaun and Colin, who were deep in earnest discussion with their heads in the engine of the car, when she saw Prunes slinking round the corner of the boxes, dragging something which looked suspiciously like a bridle. Christine flung open her window, and yelled, but Shaun and Colin had started the engine, and did not hear. She threw her towel on to her bed, raced downstairs, and out into the yard, her short hair dripping down her neck.

Prunes had vanished, and Christine tore round the

the side of the boxes. She scrambled through the fence into the paddock, and spotted him having a tug-of-war with Punch. They had Jack's bridle between them. Seeing her coming, both dogs let go, and flew off across the paddock. Christine picked up the bridle in horror.

It was covered in mud, the curb chain had vanished, and there were tooth-marks all over the leather.

Christine raced back into the yard with it, threw it into the tack room, and picked up the tack bucket, which was still half full of cold, dirty water. She would have to boil some more water, and it was getting dark already. Luckily there was a light in the tack room. She switched it on, and was about to go up to the house for the water when Colin walked in.

"What on earth is that?" he asked, seeing the bridle.

"Jack's bridle," replied Christine. She explained what had happened. "It must have got knocked down or something. Trust Prunes to find it," she finished. "And I've still got to dry my hair, and iron my shirt, and clean my shoes, and steam my hat. I'll never get it all done, and the Major will be furious when he sees this, especially the tooth marks."

"I'll do it," offered Colin. "If you'll iron my shirt as well, and sew that button on my jacket."

"Willingly," agreed Christine, who was sick of cleaning tack.

She handed the bucket to Colin, and went back into the house. Alison met her on the doorstep.

"There's a telephone call for Shaun," she said. "Has he gone?"

"No," replied Christine.

She shouted, and Shaun appeared, covered in engine oil, saddle soap, and horse hairs.

"There's a 'phone call for you," Alison told him. "Long distance."

Shaun thanked her, and dashed into the house. Christine went upstairs to dry her hair, and Alison wandered out, combing her hair in a half-hearted way, to see what Colin was doing.

Ten minutes later Shaun appeared. He looked extremely excited.

"What's happened?" asked Alison, looking up from

the reins she was cleaning. "Been left a fortune?"

"Better than that," replied Shaun. "I've been offered a wonderful job."

"Doing what?" asked Alison curiously.

"Driving racing cars for a French firm," answered Shaun. "They want me to fly over next week."

"I didn't know you raced," said Colin, with interest, stopping soaping the nose band.

"Yes, it's my job," replied Shaun. "At least, at the moment I'm testing, not racing. I was longing for a chance like this. If I do well, I shall be driving for them all over the world."

"Are they a big firm?" asked Colin.

"Fairly," replied Shaun. "It's the Du Monde motor works, near Paris."

"Yes, I've heard of them," said Colin. "Their cars do well, don't they?"

"Yes," agreed Shaun.

"What about Toreador?" asked Alison.

"I don't know," Shaun looked thoughtful. "I can't very well take him with me, because I shan't be stopping in one place for very long. I suppose I could leave him here. I expect I shall come to England quite often."

"You could leave him here, at Stone Heath," suggested Alison.

"Yes. My contract is only for a year. Then, if I don't make the grade, I shall be coming back, I suppose," replied Shaun. "But who would ride him?"

"I expect Edna would," suggested Colin.

"She might manage him," agreed Shaun, who had no idea whether Edna Blythe was any good or not.

"Christine managed him all right," Alison pointed out. "All the way back from Midgely."

"Yes, of course, she did," agreed Shaun. "I could try it, anyway, if she agrees."

"Will you still be able to jump him to-morrow?" asked Alison.

"Oh yes," answered Shaun. "I shan't be leaving until about next Wednesday, anyway."

He glanced at his watch. "I must go now!" he exclaimed. "See you early to-morrow. Goodnight."

He got into his car, and shot out of the yard in his usual fashion.

"I wonder if Edna will take Toreador on," said Alison.

"She can't for some time," Colin pointed out.

"But the Major might ride him until she's better," suggested Alison. "Or Mrs. Pollitzer."

Colin agreed.

They worked in silence for a little longer, whilst, outside, the light faded, and the wind sent clouds scudding across the sky. The electric light flickered, and Colin glanced at the bulb.

"I hope it'll last," he said, looking back at the half cleaned bridle.

"I must iron my shirt, and press my tie," said Alison,

looking up. "Can you finish this?"

"I suppose I shall have to," replied Colin. He looked more closely at the bridle. "By the way, where's the curb chain?"

"Isn't it there?" Alison looked at the empty curb hooks, and then felt in the bucket of dirty tack water.

"I wonder what has happened to it?" Colin looked round the tack room.

At that moment Christine appeared in the doorway, her short brown hair now dry, and looking fluffy at the ends.

"Did you find the curb chain?" she asked, seeing that they had not finished.

"No. Why, is it lost?" asked Colin. "We saw that it wasn't on the bridle, but we thought it must be somewhere about."

"The dogs lost it, outside somewhere," answered Christine. "It may be anywhere in the yard."

"And it's pitch dark," said Alison, staring out in horror. "Oh help! What will the Major say if he hasn't got a curb chain on his bridle to-morrow?"

"I'll fetch some torches. We shall have to find it," said Colin.

He dashed off, and Alison told Christine about Shaun.

"Poor Edna. Fancy getting landed with Toreador," said Christine. "Though he was good coming home from Midgely."

"It was probably the only time in his life that he had been good," said Alison discouragingly.

Colin arrived with the torches, and they went out into the yard. They started at the tack room door, and hunted carefully, keeping in line, down to the corner of the boxes, and into the paddock. They had been searching for nearly half an hour when Alison suddenly saw something glinting silver in the torchlight. She pounced, and held up the missing curb chain.

They carried it back triumphantly to the tack room, and Colin finished the bridle while Alison and Christine pressed and ironed all their clothes for the next day.

They went to bed at last, when it was almost midnight. Edna had gone long ago, and left them to it, knowing from long experience that it would take them half the night to get ready. Alison set her alarm clock for six o'clock, and fell asleep the moment she lay down.

147

Chapter Eleven

SHOW DAY AT LAST

IT seemed only a few minutes before the shrill ringing of her blue alarm clock woke Alison on the morning of the show. She lay for a moment, trying to remember what was happening. Then, in a sudden burst of excitement and fright, she realised that to-day she would ride Trix round the jumps in the ring, and race her in the gymkhana events.

Alison dived out of bed, and hung out of the window, breathing the cool, sweet air. It was a wonderful day. The sky was clear, and there was a thick mist over the paddock and the heath beyond it.

Christine was also awake, sitting up, and demanding to know what the weather was like. Alison told her, as she dressed herself in her old slacks, shirt and shoes ready for work.

They hammered on Colin's door on the way down, let the dogs out, and raced across the yard to the stables. The horses were surprised to see them so early, and they whickered in a friendly, curious fashion as the two girls seized pitch forks and began to muck out at top speed.

Presently Colin joined them, and began to follow them round with fresh straw. When the beds and mucking out were done, they watered and gave the horses a short feed each. Then Shaun's car swung into the yard, and he offered to run them down to the farm to fetch Morning, Storm, Dolly and Biscuit. They accepted gladly, grabbed halters from the tack room, being careful to close the door after them to prevent the dogs repeating yesterday's performance, and dived into Shaun's car.

They caught the horses without trouble, and led them back to the stables in Shaun's dusty wake. They arrived to find him filling hay nets for the horses to munch while they were being groomed.

They put the youngsters, Dolly and Biscuit into the sheds, and rushed in to breakfast, taking Shaun with them. They were all hungry after their early morning work, and they ate a huge breakfast before tearing out again to start grooming.

Elsie and John had arrived, and started on their own mounts, while the others, including Shaun, began the rest. Luckily the stable ponies had kept fairly clean, but the four who were turned out were covered in mud. Major Davidson and Mrs. Pollitzer were next to arrive. The Major groomed Jack, and Mrs. Pollitzer did Goldie, as Christine had Morning to do when she had finished Albatross.

Alison was plaiting Trix, and kept pricking her fingers, and losing the needle. The chestnut fidgeted and shook her head, almost knocking Alison off her upturned bucket. Alison had plaited before, with rubber bands but

Alison was plaiting Trix

never for a show, and never with cotton. She did two plaits, and started a third, feeling rather dissatisfied with the first, though the second was not too bad.

Christine thanked her lucky stars that Albatross was hogged, and started to groom Morning. Colin was plaiting Oberon, and Elsie was making a rather unsuccessful attempt to plait Melody.

John was still grooming Puck, very glad that he had no mane. Shaun was not attempting to plait his stallion, as he knew what Toreador's reaction would probably be, and anyway, he looked better with it loose.

Alison finished Trix at last, and went to help Elsie with Melody. Colin was half-way through Storm, and Mrs. Pollitzer had finished Goldie, and was helping Christine to finish Morning, who was being awkward about having his mane done. They were leaving Storm's loose, as it was very thick, and bristly where she had rubbed it.

By nine o'clock all the ponies were tacked up, and Dolly and her foal were ready for the trailer which Edna had booked to take them to the show.

"Well, are we all ready?" asked Christine, at last, when everyone had changed into their best riding clothes, and presented Edna with their lunches, mackintoshes, head collars, and feeds for the ponies.

Colin rode Oberon and led Morning, Christine rode Albatross and led Storm, Alison rode Trix and led Melody, Elsie rode Goldie, John rode Puck, Shaun, of

151

course, had Toreador, and Major Davidson rode Jack. The Major led, with Shaun close behind him. Next came John and Elsie, followed by Alison, Christine, and Colin bringing up the rear. The ride should take just over an hour, as the show ground was by the sea, on the other side of Midgely.

As they rode through the outskirts of the town they began to see signs of the show everywhere. Horse-boxes and cattle-trucks roared past. Cars, station-wagons, jeeps, traps, and lorries flashed by, crowded with people and dogs. The fruit and flowers had gone earlier, but there was a dog show, and the animals that passed ranged from aristocratic dachshunds, corgies, poodles, and alsatians, to shaggy mongrels and lurchers, and small farm terriers. They passed a group of riders, a man on a tall chestnut, with a girl on a roan cob and a small boy on a black shetland, and a few minutes later they were passed by a man and woman on a showy bay and a pretty grey. The woman was riding side-saddle.

"Competition for you, Alison," shouted Christine. "I'll bet she's in the hack class."

"Oh help!" yelled Alison, patting Trix's hard red neck.

They rode on through Midgely, following the sign which said, TO THE SHOW. Then they came in sight of the ground, with its marquees, flags, bunting, the big circus tent behind the rest, and the various roofs, wheels, towers, and scaffolding of the fair. Mrs. Pollitzer's old car passed them slowly, with Edna hanging out of the window to ask if everything was all right, and the dogs barking excitedly on the back seat. It was followed by a Land Rover pulling the trailer carrying Dolly and Biscuit.

A few moments later they arrived at the entrance marked, COMPETITORS ONLY.

They filed through, and found themselves on the show ground. Toreador was terribly excited. He pressed his nose right in to his chest, lifting his feet very high off the ground, and snorted every time he put a foot down. Jack jogged sideways, and goggled at the white tent that housed the gate man, and shied at the car park, which was next to it. The ground was already crowded, although there were almost twenty minutes before the first class was due to start.

The children made their way through the people, tents, horses, cars, and animals to the horse-boxes, where they found the trailer which housed Dolly and Biscuit.

Edna and Mrs. Pollitzer were waiting for them, and when they reached them the riders flung themselves off their ponies, took off saddles, and began to brush over Goldie, Oberon, and Puck, who were in the first class, which was the showing class for heath ponies under saddle. Puck was very excited, and he would not stand still. He fidgeted and walked round in circles, making John walk after him as he tried to brush his tail. Mrs. Pollitzer went to the rescue, and saddled the restless pony for him while Edna brushed him down. Colin and Christine brushed each other's coat, saddled up their ponies, and mounted.

Shaun had dismounted, and was having a job with Toreador, who was whirling round him in circles and rearing. When the stallion had trodden on his toe about six times Shaun decided to remount, and ride him round for a time to calm him down. Alison, who had brushed Trix down by now, offered to accompany him, as Trix's first class followed the heath ponies, and she was almost as excited as the stallion.

Elsie unsaddled Melody, and began to brush her over, and Storm and Morning watched everything with wide, startled eyes. They were tied to the side of the trailer, alongside Jack, who was being unsaddled, and having his sheet put on, as his class was not until quite late in the afternoon.

Colin, Christine and John, the three who were in the first class rode off towards the ring, while Shaun and Alison rode away in the other direction, towards an open part of the ground where other people were exercising their horses.

The collecting ring was crowded, with a very mixed selection of ponies ranging from a beautiful little chestnut thoroughbred, who did not look as though he had ever seen the heath, to several old, ragged ponies with mud still clinging to their coats, who had obviously only just been taken from it.

The three children filed through the gap in the ropes, and began to ride slowly round the collecting ring, examining their fellow competitors with interest. Puck danced and bounced, upsetting several strange ponies as he sidled past, but his two companions walked calmly enough, keeping an interested eye on everything, but too used to shows to get excited.

In another ring, past the flower tent, heavy horses were being judged. In another part of the ground were the pens of pigs, sheep, and cattle, in yet another part was the dog show, and a long tent housed rabbits, mice, and caged birds. Every animal that was kept on or around the heath seemed to be present, and the noise was deafening. Barking, lowing, whinnying, bleating, the sound of cars and tractors, a roar from one of the circus lions, and the sound of people talking, laughing, calling, and cheering went on incessantly.

At last the judges appeared, the steward pulled the rope away from the entrance, and the first class filed into the ring.

It had been decided beforehand that once in the ring, Christine, John and Colin should separate, so that their ponies would not be too close together, in case they decided to be nappy. Edna, who was installed in her seat, on one of the iron chairs ranged round one end of the ring for the more wealthy members of the audience, was pleased to see that all three ponies looked well turned out, and their riders were making them walk out, except

155

for Puck, who, of course, was jogging and pulling.

They walked round three times, during which a nice-looking grey pony kicked the old bay behind him, and Puck settled down a bit. Then they were told to trot on. The leader, a girl with fair plaits, riding a showy skewbald, led on at an extended trot. Puck gave three bucks and shot past four ponies on the inside before John managed to stop him, and Goldie and Oberon trotted on quite well, though Oberon was pulling because he wanted to pass the black pony in front of him. Then they were told to canter, and Puck shot off again, upsetting the chestnut thoroughbred, who began to buck and sent his rider over his head. Goldie led off on the right leg, with a lot of work from Christine to keep her up to her bridle, but Oberon went disunited, dropped back into a trot, and then, when Colin persuaded him to lead properly, he was unbalanced. His nose stuck out, and his hocks trailed.

Then they were told to walk, and change the rein. They repeated the walk, trot, and canter, and then, when they were walking again, the judges began to call them in. First a nice-looking bay, a typical heath pony, then, in quick succession, a dun mare, a black gelding, the skewbald, Goldie, and a bay mare. Then the judges hesitated, before calling in Oberon, and last of all another bay, who was not very spectacular, though he had no glaring faults, but was very well schooled.

Then the rest of the class was sent into the back row, and the front line stood as well as the riders could persuade them, whilst the judges examined them. Then they had to canter, a figure of eight, dismount, mount again, and gallop on round the ring. The bay changed places with the dun, and the skewbald moved up to third, and Goldie to fourth. That was the order in which they stayed, and Christine rode triumphantly out with the green rosette, to be congratulated by the rest of the Stone Heath people.

Alison was waiting in the collecting ring for the "Hack" class, having left Shaun riding the still over-excited Toreador quietly round the meadow. Trix was trembling all over with excitement as they waited to be called in, and she was sweating hard. The rest of the party watched from the ropes, holding their ponies.

"Poor Alison," remarked Colin, as the class entered the ring with Trix cantering on the spot.

"She's going to have a rough ride," agreed Christine, patting Goldie for the hundredth time.

Most of the women in the class were riding side-saddle, and the horses were mostly tall, fine-boned thoroughbreds. Trix, in her snaffle and drop noseband, and her hunting saddle, looked odd beside the double bridles and straight cut show saddles of the rest of the competitors. She was the wrong type, too, with the obvious Arabian breeding in her head, hind quarters, and small, compact build. Her stride was shorter, and more springy —not long and smooth—and she was far too fresh. She cantered sideways, bucking and bouncing, throwing Alison on to her neck. When they started to canter she took off, and flew round the ring, upsetting several horses, and making one elegant thoroughbred jump the ropes and vanish into the distance, much to the judges' fury. In the end Alison brought her out, and took her back to the box, to attempt to calm her down a bit before the "Best Rider" class, which was next.

Christine arrived, just as Alison was about to re-mount, and offered her Goldie. Alison hesitated for a moment, then, after looking at Trix's streaming flanks and wild eye, she accepted. Christine started to lead Trix in circles in an attempt to cool her down.

The "Best Rider" class entered the ring sitting self-consciously straight, with their toes as far up as they would go, and their knees tightly in. Puck, as usual, spoilt John's efforts by bouncing, and throwing John out of the saddle at each bound. Melody, too, was rather excited, and when they were told to do a sitting trot she threw Elsie about rather, as she was riding too stiffly.

Alison rode as well as she knew how, and Goldie co-operated beautifully. Alison was astonished to find herself called in second, in which place she stayed. Goldie cantered out of the ring with the blue and the green rosettes flapping from her brow band, to be greeted with carrots and congratulations from everyone.

The next class was "Heath Bred Mares With Foal At Foot." Colin was waiting in the ring entrance with a sleepy, placid Dolly, and Christine had the bouncy, excited Biscuit. There were a dozen entries, which included a foal that was almost a yearling, a beautiful grey part-bred Arab mare, with a foal who looked pure Arab, and a piebald mare with a pure white foal with a black patch over one eye. Biscuit held his own well against the other foals, and Dolly, well-groomed and fit, matched the other mares well. They were brought in third, where they stayed, receiving the yellow rosette.

Alison was waiting in the collecting ring with Storm, and she took Dolly from Colin as he came out, and handed him the grey filly's reins. It was a big class, and Storm was rather nervous. She went in fits and starts, one moment dragging, the next moment almost pulling Colin over. They were finally placed fifth, and given the white rosette for Highly Commended.

The next event was the "Backed This Year" class and soon Christine was in the collecting ring on Morning, with Alison holding him. Colin took over the leading rein, and they entered the ring with ten other young horses, most of whom were pulling and sidling excitedly. Morning took one look at the ring, with its watching crowds, shining cars parked at the ropes, and jumps piled round the sides, and tried to turn round. Colin hung on, and Christine urged him gently forward. They managed to enter the ring, and began to circle the judges. One bay colt got away from the girl who was leading him, started bucking, got rid of his rider, and charged out of the ring. Red Morning watched him go with interest, and Colin tightened his hold on the lead rein, as the filly in front shied and kicked out at nothing in particular. None of the youngsters was very good-looking. Morning was about the best there.

They had to trot, and he behaved very well, in spite of the black filly in front of him cantering and trying to shy.

Morning was called in first, and stayed there. They left the ring happily, with the red rosette clashing horribly with Morning's red coat.

Christine hastily mounted Albatross for the "Hunter" class, which was not divided into light-weight, middle-weight, and heavy-weight, though a special rosette was given for the best of each type. Albatross was his usual, steady self, even when asked to gallop, and with horses shooting past him on all sides when they were asked to pull up. He kept his head, and came quietly back to a walk before several showy light-weights and a heavy-weight bay had begun to slow down. But he was older than most of the others, and his legs were scarred. He was called into the front row, but no one expected him to get a rosette, until the chestnut horse standing fifth ran away with the judge. The judge tried Albatross next, and was delighted. Albatross left the ring with the white rosette. The middle-weight rosette was awarded to the horse standing third, a brown mare.

The next class was the showing under fourteen two, and it was mostly made up of miniature thoroughbreds, and Anglo-Arabs. The Scotts had nothing entered, so they returned to the trailer, where they unsaddled their ponies, and unpacked their lunch. Edna joined them, when the class was over, and reported that the chestnut who had bucked his rider off in the Heath showing had won. Shaun brought Toreador back, and unsaddled him, but he said that the stallion was still very excited.

They ate their lunch sitting on the grass by the trailer, watching the continuous coming and going of people and animals, though many people were either having lunch in the marquee, or eating sandwiches on the grass. The air was full of the smells that always accompany a show, trampled grass, animals, petrol, and the smell of the sea carried on the wind. It was a glorious day, though rather hotter than they would have chosen. The sky was cloudless, and the breeze warm. The horses munched their feeds contentedly, and even Trix and Toreador seemed quieter. They had been given their feeds earlier, as they had to jump straight after the lunch interval.

Alison was beginning to feel nervous, and she had visions of Trix jumping the ropes, or galloping out of the ring. Shaun, too, was growing nervous, and he kept glancing at Toreador, who was watching everything that went on with intense interest.

Then the loud-speaker suddenly stopped playing music, crackled crazily for a moment, went silent, and then suddenly came back to life.

"Will all competitors for the 'Local Novice Jumping' please go to the collecting ring," it said.

Alison and Shaun jumped up, and grabbed their saddles. Trix blew herself out, and Toreador cow-kicked at Shaun. When it came to bridling, Trix decided to be awkward, and stuck her head in the air. Colin came to Alison's rescue, and between them they got her bridled and ready. Then the two riders mounted, and Edna started back to her seat.

Shaun and Alison rode across the show ground to the ring with Trix and Toreador pulling and jogging. The rest of the Stone Heath people followed.

Competitors were arriving from all over the ground, on horses of all shapes and sizes, from a sixteen hand thoroughbred, with a curb bit, to several grass-fat heath ponies.

People stared at Toreador in surprise, for he was an unusual type of horse to find even in a jumping class, where so many odd horses appear. His seal-brown coat shone, sliding over his muscles as he moved. He lifted his fore-feet high above the ground, his crest, arched-tail carried high, and long mane flowing over his shoulders. He shook his head, flinging drops of white foam over his chest and shoulders, and over Shaun's boots. His lovely, fiery eyes shone, and his little ears pricked sharply. Shaun wore a bowler, black coat, breeches, and boots, but he still managed to look like an Irish gipsy.

Trix's red coat glowed in the fierce sun, one of her plaits was coming undone, and she looked more Arabian than ever as she danced towards the ring. She had dried off after the morning, and Alison had brushed her over, making her look much better than she had done before lunch. Alison wore a black coat that had once belonged to Christine, and which was getting rather worn, jodhpurs, and a black crash cap. Neither rider wore gloves, or carried a stick, as they both knew that they would need their hands free, and that it would take them all their time to stay in the ring.

The jumps were up, the highest at three feet three.

"They ought to be able to jump those," remarked Alison, patting Trix's slightly damp neck.

"Yes, but the trouble is, will they?" asked Shaun, as Toreador plunged excitedly.

Alison shook her head.

They entered the collecting ring, and sat looking at their fellow competitors. The most formidable looking were a grey cob, ridden by a tall, thin boy with glasses, a brown thoroughbred mare, ridden by a small, slim girl of about sixteen, and a skewbald mare, ridden by a well-known show jumping rider, a man of about thirty, with very short stirrups, plaited nylon reins, and a jumping saddle.

At last the steward called the first competitors, a girl on a black cob, into the ring. She had three refusals at the first jump, and was followed by the professional man on the skewbald, who got clear as far as the exit, where the skewbald turned suddenly nappy, and started to rear. It went up four times, and then the fifth time it went too high, lost its balance, and fell sideways. Its rider jumped off, and it scrambled to its feet at once, but they were eliminated.

Horse after horse jumped, none doing very well, and then it was Shaun's turn. Toreador entered the ring with a bound, took one look at the crowd, and tried to dive out again. Shaun managed to prevent that, and was told to start.

Chapter Twelve

COVERED IN GLORY

THE first jump was a low brush with wings. The stallion tore at it much too fast, cleared it with an unnecessarily large leap, and galloped towards the second jump, the gate. Shaun tried frantically to steady him, but they were in mid-air, and over. Shaun landed on the stallion's neck, and lost both stirrups as they tore at the third jump, the parallel bars. Toreador cleared it by at least two feet, Shaun riding without stirrups, and hoping for the best, and the crowd cheered as the stallion raced round the corner and charged the fourth jump, the road closed. Here, surprised by the lamps which hung from it, and the flags at either end, Toreador jumped even higher than usual, and landed far out on the other side, with Shaun almost off. Now he took off in earnest, and as Shaun tried frantically to get some control over him, he went at the in-and-out at a flat-out gallop. He took off for the first jump in a huge leap, and tried to take the second as well, failed, landed on the second part, almost fell, managed to keep on his feet, and they flew down towards the triple bars, which the stallion cleared perfectly. He landed with his head down, and started to buck. Shaun came off at the second, but he hung on to the stallion, and led him out of the ring to noisy applause from the spectators, who thought it the most entertaining round that they had ever seen.

"If he hadn't tried to take the in-and-out as one, and then bucked you off, he'd have had a clear round," said Colin, as Shaun appeared.

"Never mind, he certainly gave everyone something for their money," grinned Shaun, patting the hot, dark neck.

"He's a wonderful jumper," said Christine admiringly. "Everyone round us thought so."

"You had your photograph taken as you came over the road closed," said Colin. "It should be a good one."

They looked back at the ring in time to see a roan cob complete a mediocre round, then Trix cantered into the ring with her nose in the air, and a wild light in her eye.

"Poor Alison," said Christine, for the second time that day, as she saw her cousin's set face as that youngster wrestled with the chestnut.

Alison was told to start, and to everyone's astonishment she and Trix cleared the first jump perfectly, if rather fast. They cleared jump after jump, going very fast, but it was obvious that Alison still had plenty of control. They cleared the in-and-out perfectly, and raced down the centre of the ring to the triple, Alison with her eyes fixed on the jump, judging the take-off. Trix jumped at exactly the right moment, cleared it with ease, and galloped out of the ring with the first clear round that day.

Trix went half-way across the show ground before Alison could stop her, but then they turned and Alison rode her slowly back to the others, patting the mare, and praising her. There were no more clear rounds. Alison had won the "Local Novice Jumping."

Later, Trix took advantage of Alison having her hands full with the cup, and took off. She galloped all the way back to the trailer, and Alison dropped the cup on the way. It arrived at the trailer just after she did, carried by the fair girl on the skewbald, who had been third in the heath ponies showing, and who introduced herself as Marcelle Crey. Her pony's name was Actress.

The next class was the "Fourteen Two Jumping," which came between the two novice classes, to give people who were competing in both a chance to rest their horses. John was fourth, with six faults. Puck had calmed down a lot, as John had been riding him round since lunch time, keeping him walking and trotting slowly. Marcelle and Actress were first.

Then Shaun took Toreador back into the collecting ring for the "Open Novice" class. The course was the same as it had been for the "Local Novice," except for the gate and the road closed, which were now three feet six, and for the fact that a three-foot red wall had been added. When Shaun's turn came, there had so far been no clear rounds. Toreador entered the ring a little more calmly this time.

Shaun was given the signal to start, and the stallion

plunged forward into a gallop, and was over the brush almost without bothering about it. As before, his speed increased, and he flew over the gate, in spite of the extra three inches. Then the parallel bars—a huge spring, and he was over. The wall was next. Toreador did not hesitate; he jumped perfectly, and plunged on towards the road closed. Another huge leap; Shaun lost his hat, which hit the stallion's quarters. He kicked out, shot sideways, and came flying up to the in-and-out at an angle. He jumped awkwardly, almost hit the first jump, cleared the second by a fraction, and landed Shaun almost on his ears. They galloped towards the last jump. Shaun had dropped his reins, and he had no stirrups. Up, and over. Clear! They tore past the finishing post, and out of the ring. Shaun had been completely unseated by the last jump, and he was rapidly slipping sideways. As they left the ring he let go altogether, and landed on the grass under the horse's feet. Everyone who was close enough to see what was happening gasped in horror for it looked as though Toreador would tread on him. But the horse avoided him neatly, and shot away across the ground, scattering people and horses in all directions, pursued by a man on an ugly black hunter with a surprising turn of speed.

Shaun scrambled up, grabbed Puck off John, who had been watching, and dashed off in pursuit of his horse, who was slowing himself up by kicking and bucking. Shaun's feet almost touched the ground, but he was not heavy, and Puck scuttled along as fast as he could, surprised and pleased at being asked to gallop after so much restriction, and being made to do slow canters.

The man on the black was alongside the stallion now, and instead of going faster when he heard his pursuer

coming Toreador skidded to a stop, and swung round to see what was happening.

The black also stopped dead, and his rider grabbed the stallion's reins, and swung his horse out of the way as

Toreador reared. Then Puck scuttled up, and Shaun sprang off him, and took Toreador's reins from the man, who offered to lead Puck back to the ring. Shaun thanked him gladly, mounted Toreador, and followed him.

Shaun arrived just in time to hear himself announced as winner of the novice jumping, and he rode across to receive his rosette and cup. Toreador was feeling pleased with himself, and he bucked and plunged as he led the canter round. Shaun hung on to him, and managed to keep him under some control, and avoid dropping the cup, which the others in the party took from him as soon as he could persuade Toreador to stand still long enough for him to hand it to them.

The next class was the Open Jumping. Major Davidson had taken Jack for a canter round, and was now walking him round the collecting ring. The Stone Heath party watched tensely as the class started, and in the first six horses there were three clear rounds—the well-known man, who had ridden the skewbald in the Local class, on his bay mare, Wood Wind, a woman on a light chestnut mare called Laburnum, and a girl on a grey gelding called Silver Sand. Then it was the Major's turn. Jack entered the ring at a very slow, collected canter, perfectly under control, very different from the way he had gone with Christine on their first day at Stone Heath. Major Davidson was an expert rider, and he proceeded to demonstrate how a round should be jumped. He and Jack cleared every fence in perfect time

170

with each other, increasing their speed at exactly the right moment, and jumping just high enough to clear everything safely.

Altogether there were six clear rounds, and the jumps were raised for the jump off. Jack was fourth to jump, after Wood Wind, Laburnum, and Silver Sand had all had faults. Again they jumped a perfect round. Both the other horses made faults. Jack had won the Open Jumping.

The whole party congratulated the Major, and fed Jack on carrots and sugar. Then they suddenly realised that the loud-speaker was calling for all competitors for the "Juvenile Bending." Alison, John, and Elsie dashed off to fetch their ponies. Alison was riding Trix, although Christine had offered to lend her Goldie. There were a lot of entries, and a lot of heats. Alison was in the third. Trix was very excited. She refused to stand still at the start, bucked, and spun round in circles, plunged forward, and tried to kick the pony next to her. When she was facing in the right direction at last the steward shouted, "Go."

All five ponies leapt forward, and Trix led as they reached the first pole. Alison had expected her to be awkward, although she had practised hard enough, but the little chestnut behaved perfectly. She bent at a fast gallop, turned at the end like a polo pony, and came racing back, bending round the poles like a copper-coloured snake. She was leading by three poles, and she galloped flat out past the winning post and out of the ring before Alison could stop her.

Elsie won her heat, but Puck got excited, and knocked down two poles. Then they reached the semi-finals. Again, both Elsie and Alison won their heats, and they lined up for the final with the other two finalists, a small, handy grey pony, ridden by a boy of about eleven, and an excitable bay mare ridden by a girl with red hair.

Trix jumped straight into the lead for the third time, and won easily. Elsie and the grey pony fought it out for second place, as the bay knocked down a pole. The grey pony just beat Melody by about a head.

In the senior bending Colin and Oberon managed to get into third place behind a girl on a showy strawberry roan, and a boy on a tall, weedy bay thoroughbred.

Trix was in the first heat of the potato race, again very excited. When they were told to start she shot forward again, bent beautifully all the way up the row of poles, turned neatly at the top, and bent beautifully all the way home, ignoring Alison's pleas for her to stop at the potatoes on top of each pole.

Christine, to her own surprise, was first, with a stranger second, and John third.

The sack race was next. Trix was horrified at the bare idea of approaching such a dangerous looking object as an empty sack, and she shied, and edged away. When Alison finally got off and tried to lead her up she reared, pulled the reins out of Alison's hands, and charged out of the ring and across to the trailer, where she was caught by a helpful onlooker, and led back to the collecting ring.

None of them won anything in the sack race, and then came the last class of the show, the "Open Musical Poles." They were all entered except Shaun and the Major, and they cantered happily round the ring, listening carefully to the music.

The sun was setting in a blaze of colour. People were collecting their children, horses, and dogs, and setting out for home. The crowd round the ropes was thinning. The professional people who had only come for the showing or jumping had left. The air was cool and fresh, and filled with the scents of the show ground after the long hot day—animals, grass, leather, and flowers. The light was fading, and long shadows were falling across the show ground. The steam roundabout was blaring its music into the evening, and people were eating chips and vinegar, bought from the stall by the gates. The circus tent was filling up for the second performance, the voice of the barker adding to the noise. Mixed with the blaring roundabout, the hunting songs and marches for the "Musical Poles," and the sounds of the circus, came the murmur of the sea, and the sleepy songs of birds.

Christine was so busy listening to the music from the loud-speaker, and watching the scene on the untidy show ground, that she completely forgot she was in a competition. The music stopped, everyone dived for poles, and Christine went on quietly cantering round the

ring, watching the glow of light from the circus tent, the
fairy lights in the trees, and the coloured lights on the
roundabout. A shout of laughter from what remained
of the audience brought her down to earth, and she
cantered out of the ring, grinning sheepishly.

Colin was out shortly after Christine, and Elsie soon
followed him. John managed to get reserve, and Alison,
riding with grim concentration while everyone else
relaxed and enjoyed themselves, managed to win, in spite
of Trix's excitement.

As Alison led the canter round to the gay music
from the last part of the Overture to William Tell she
thought how wonderful the day had been. It was the
first show at which she had won so much, and Trix had
been wonderful. And she had always wanted to win a
jumping class.

Behind her, with the blue second, came Marcelle,
with Actress doing a beautiful collected canter. Third
was the showy strawberry roan, and fourth came Puck,
still bouncing, with his bristly red crest arched, and his
white face showing up in the twilight.

Alison and John rode straight across the emptying
ground to the trailer, where Dolly and Biscuit were
allowed a last look round before starting for home.

Head collars, summer sheets, mackintoshes, and
grooming kit were collected and either piled into the
trailer, or into Mrs. Pollitzer's car, together with Punch
and Prunes, who had been surprisingly good all day.

Prunes had got fourth in the class for the best conditioned dog, and Punch had a third in the farm terrier class.

Shaun saddled Toreador, and mounted, and the others mounted their ponies. The Major mounted Jack, and they followed the trailer as it bumped slowly over the rough ground towards the gate, out of which was pouring a steady stream of cars, vans, cattle trucks, and horse-boxes. Mrs. Pollitzer followed them in her car, with Prunes and Punch balancing precariously on the back seat, their noses bumping the side windows with every lurch.

Once through the gate the trailer and the car went on ahead, and the riders made their way quietly through the lighted town among the rest of the show traffic. They passed Marcelle, who was accompanied by a girl on a bicycle, enough like her to be her sister, with her carrier piled with mackintosh and head collar, and grooming kit in her basket. The strawberry roan and the grey pony passed them at a fast trot, their riders discussing the show in loud voices, waving their arms about, and making Trix, Toreador, and the youngsters jog and bounce.

Once through the town the road became quiet, the only sound the clatter of the ponies' hooves, and an occasional car. It was quite dark by now, and the stars were out. Behind them they could still see the glow over the show ground, and the breeze carried faint sounds of music.

"Wasn't it a good show," remarked Alison, turning

in her saddle and peering through the gloom at Morning's white star and Albatross's pale coat.

"Yes, lovely," agreed Christine. "I did feel an idiot in the 'Musical Poles', though."

"You were looking at the sky and wearing a sickly smile," Alison informed her.

"I wasn't," objected Christine. "I was watching everyone getting ready to leave."

"I should have liked to see the circus," remarked Alison. "It's a shame it's only on for to-night."

"Yes, it is," agreed Colin. "It would have been worth seeing, I should think."

"Oh, well . . ." Alison patted Trix. "Wasn't she wonderful?" she said happily. "I never thought she'd jump like that."

"Nor did we," admitted Colin. "She looked as though she was trying to think up a way to get out of the ring."

"By the way, did I tell you that Edna will take Toreador on?" asked Shaun, turning in his saddle, and letting the stallion's reins lie on his neck. "She said she would love to ride him."

"Oh, good," cried Alison. "Then he'll be here for ages, and perhaps he'll do well jumping."

"Perhaps he will," agreed Shaun. "I hope I shall have time to ride him."

Suddenly, a car whizzed past them, headlights blazing, with a blast on its horn, and Toreador shied and bucked, making Jack start forward and upsetting the others.

"He'll have to reform if he's going to get far," called Shaun over his shoulder, trying to collect his reins as the horse dived forward.

They rode on through the soft, warm night. An owl hooted, and the ponies pricked their ears to listen. Bats fluttered overhead, and somewhere on the heath a fox barked.

"Do you think Edna will ask us again?" wondered Alison. "For Christmas, perhaps. They have a lot of hunting round here, I should think."

"She might," agreed Christine. "It would be lovely round here. Hardly any wire, or roads."

"Would you take Toreador, Shaun?" asked Alison.

"I might," replied his owner. "He'd probably buck me off right in the middle of Hounds!"

"That would be rather funny," replied Alison.

"For you, perhaps," retorted Shaun severely.

They rode on towards home, through Stone village, and turned into the track to the stables. The horses, thinking of home and supper, started to jog, and Trix whinnied shrilly. Dolly, who was just being led across the yard by Mrs. Pollitzer, answered. The lights were on in the stables, and the dogs dashed to meet them, barking. The horses' hooves clattered on the yard, and the riders dismounted stiffly, led the ponies in, unsaddled, and rubbed them down. The feeds were already in the mangers.

Then Alison, Colin, Christine, and Shaun walked down to the field with the ponies. They turned them loose, and watched them wander across the field in the pale moonlight, noses trailing in the cool grass. Then they turned and walked back up the road to the stables. The night was cool and clear, the dogs hunted happily in the heather, and the owl hooted again, and swooped across the road.

LIST OF TECHNICAL TERMS
USED IN THE STORY

Definitions of these terms were taken from *Summerhays' Encyclopædia for Horsemen*, by kind permission of Mr. R. S. Summerhays. (Published by F. Warne & Co. Ltd.).

BLAZE: a white marking covering most of the forehead between the eyes, and extending down the front of the face.

BRIDLE: a leather headpiece which carries the bit and reins.

CAVESSON: a headpiece used for training a young horse. It has a heavy noseband with three rings attached, to which the lunging rein can be fixed.

COW-KICK: a kick forward with the hind legs, which can be dangerous to anyone mounting, or standing beside the horse.

CURB CHAIN: a chain fitted to the eye of some bits, and arranged to lie in the groove of the jaw, just above the lower lip. The chain consists of about 17 flat links, with a ring in the centre through which the leather lip strap passes.

HALTER: a hemp headband used for young horses not broken to the bit, or for tying up in a stall.

HOGGED MANE: a term used where the mane has been wholly removed.

LIP STRAP: a thin leather strap threaded through the curb chain and buckled to the bit. The strap keeps the curb chain from overhanging the lower lip, and prevents the bit from turning.

LOOSE BOX: is usually about 10 ft. × 12 ft. and 12 ft. high. A horse stabled in a loose box does not have to be haltered and tied up, but is free to lie down, and to take limited exercise.

LUNGING: an early stage in training when, by means of a single rein attached to the bridle, the young horse can be made to circle round the trainer and learn to obey words of command.

MARTINGALE: a strap attached to the reins, bit or nose-band and used to regulate a horse's head carriage.

MUCKING OUT: Taking soiled bedding from a box or stall, and sweeping out.

OVER-REACH: is usually caused by the inner rim of the toe of the hind shoe striking against the heel of the fore-foot.

PADDOCK: an enclosed area of good quality grassland, used for rearing young horses and for turning out working animals when not required.

STALL: a compartment which is open at the rear and in which a horse must therefore be haltered.

STIRRUP IRON: a metal fitting into which the rider's foot is placed.

Edson (Printers) Ltd., Leavesden, Watford.
397/556